THE ANCESTOR TRAP

by
T.S. Falk

You want to know what is coming and get access to exclusive content?

Just write a mail to **FalkNewsletter@gmail.com** with the subject: SUBSCRIBE

TABLE OF CONTENTS

Chapter 1

Ashra Shah's office was probably the worst—and certainly the hottest, in the entire agency. To the extent that she was forced to use frozen water bottles as a rudimentary cooling system, because the air-con was broken. She would sweat so much throughout the day, she constantly needed to drink in order to stay hydrated. The fans from the three running computers only added to the heat. Maps, dots, trackers, messages from wiretaps— it was all there, an endless stream of information, so utterly irrelevant that it was almost bizarre. It seemed like some sort of punishment.

Having an uncle in the higher ranks of the agency, made her punishments even harsher, lest they be accused of nepotism. Perhaps they had just forgotten all about her, so she was doomed to watch these screens in this overheated office. Anything that distracted her was welcome; anything but the daily routine. When one of the in-house messengers brought her a small piece of paper—a wonderfully backwards method of correspondence in the age of digital communication and hacking—Ashra was delighted. She could see from the yellow paper that it was an invitation to a meeting—it was sent from the director himself.

Ashra couldn't remember the last time she had been summoned to the director's office. It had been six months since she had been called back, on the false promise that there was something only *she* could handle. She hunted black market dealers in Kathmandu. No—she didn't hunt them; that sounded way too thrilling. She *watched* them—investigating their finances, and mapping their movements. They had only become active twice, and both times, they had left the entire matter to the local police. Every day she thought about quitting and going back to London. Elliot was on her mind at all times—which was ironic, as communication between them had never fully resumed.

Something had fractured at that market in Karachi, where she had told him she would go back. Ashra often thought about how to repair that broken piece of a human relationship. She didn't know how. Fake emotions were her expertise, but real ones seemed strangely complicated.

Getting Elliot back—if that was even possible—would naturally start with her return to London; something she would do once she quit. Though quitting wasn't that easy. Every time she intended to leave, her uncle—her direct superior—asked for a few more weeks. She owed the old man her life in many ways. He had molded her into who she was now. So every time, she gave in, promising herself this would be the last time; again and again, until it was too late. By now, she was no longer sure there was anything in London she could go back to. Elliot Brand had turned his whole attention back to his hunt for an unknown, long-lost civilization they had once encountered together, and the time between their awkward video calls grew longer and longer.

They were two people living for their job and unable to share their secrets. She was bound to secrecy, and he could hardly trust the agent of a foreign government, with the details of a project like this. Especially when this woman had broken his heart in a market in Karachi—she was pretty sure that was what she had done; she had broken his heart, and he had never forgiven her. That was what she had deduced from the limited contact they had. It was quite an assumption to make, considering she had never asked him. She'd had a dozen chances, and she'd never brought up the one thing she really wanted to talk about—this strange concept they had once had, called "them." Not him and her, but *them*—a concept suddenly outdated, for the simple reason that she had let him slip through her fingers. Being with him had been precious, and she hadn't been careful. Like a dropped glass bowl that had smashed into a million pieces, she now stood in front of the shards of what had been "them," and she didn't know what to say or do to make it whole again—which resulted in her never trying.

In more lighthearted moments, Ashra laughed to herself. She had crawled through ancient ruins with him and had kept a deadly infestation from ancient times, spreading once again. That had all been easy, compared to telling him she still had feelings for him. Indeed, she was a complicated girl in a complicated situation, and that was probably too much for him.

Powering down her computers, she took a sip of water and put on a fresh shirt, before leaving her work behind to see the director. A part of her wondered if she would be fired. She had heard of budget cuts, so maybe that was why she had been summoned? She would be happy with that, actually. Her uncle wouldn't talk her out of that one. Then again, she was assured constantly how important her work was.

Now she was suddenly told, that whatever she was working on could wait, that she should report to the director right away. She did as she was told. A small intelligence agency like theirs, relied on discipline and a functioning chain of command. Nepal relied on her, as she was regularly reminded. So the director, a man who had never worked a day in the field as an agent, would see her, and maybe he wouldn't even bother to explain why she had been sidelined for half a year.

Ashra went through her options. If this turned into a performance review, she swore to herself she would quit right then and there. She made her way through the corridors of the building, that had been one of the few survivors of the devastating

3

earthquakes a few years ago. The director was easy to find—he had the only bureau guarded by a secretary.

Ashra handed the small yellow paper, without a word to Tashani, the young, attractive secretary. The women gave a sigh, gesturing toward the heavy wooden door behind her.

A large bronze label said: DIRECTOR.

They hadn't added his name, which Ashra had always considered as a sign that his position was expendable. Whoever moved into the office next, wouldn't even have to change the label.

She knocked and heard a voice behind the door. She couldn't make out the words, but from the intonation she assumed he'd asked her to enter. Opening the door to the largest bureau in the building, she stepped inside; the smell of the old, wooden furniture filled her nostrils. A couch and chairs in the corner looked like antiques, but they were not the source of the smell. The wooden panels and the humidity of the building, didn't go well together. Ashra folded her hands behind her back and stood before the sizeable desk made of mahogany wood, that filled one side of the room.

"Director Koirala, I was told to report to you."

The small, overweight man raised his eyes from a file he held. His index finger pushed his horned-rimmed glasses up on his nose, as he looked at her from head to toe. Ashra no longer cared for the dress code, as she had little contact outside her small office; she was wearing sneakers, jeans, and a black shirt. The director didn't comment on her casual attire, and instead gave her a smile that seemed cold.

"Agent Shah, good to see you." His words and his tone did not match. "Your uncle speaks so highly of you. The job you did in those ruins out there in the Himalayas and all that."

"Thank you, sir."

"Too bad you brought no proof of your findings."

"Yes, sir."

"Some even think you might have made up the whole story." He pulled his glasses off and leaned back.

"Does that include the present . . . director?" Ashra asked, unfolding her hands.

"It's my job to receive information and doubt it. I question every report, every fact, and openly measure them by the proof provided. What I believe . . . well, let's say I can't afford something like a belief. Which is why I haven't acted on behalf of that information. Which is *also* why I made every effort to verify your findings. So far, it seems the only proof is the witness report of your friend and former lover, Professor Elliot Brand, who we accept as a reliable source." The director waved his glasses. "We aren't here to discuss alien ruins though."

"They weren't alien, Director. My report says pretty clearly—"

"May it be as it is. As I said, that's not our topic."

"Then what is our topic, Director?" She knew she wasn't in a position to push for an answer, but she was losing her patience.

"The point is, someone believes you." The director leaned forward and tapped on the files he had just read.

"Someone?"

5

"Someone from the CIA." He raised his brows.

"CIA?" Ashra asked. He now had her full attention. It wasn't often they discussed the matter of the Central Intelligence Agency of the United States of America in these halls.

"Yes. As you know, we have several fields of cooperation with the guys from Langley. Terror financing, persons of interest. We exchange notes on several topics." The director said.

"As do almost all intelligence agencies in the world, yes," Ashra said, taking away the delusions of the man that their little National Investigation Bureau had any special connection to the largest intelligence agency in the world.

"Yes, of course." The director gave her the briefest of smiles. He put his glasses on again; a gesture perhaps meant to give his words additional gravity.

"So, what's this about?" Ashra asked.

"The CIA contacted us through our channels, requesting our assistance."

"Our assistance?" Ashra almost laughed but managed to limit her reaction to a frown instead.

"Yes, unusual, isn't it?" The director agreed. "I can't remember this happening since we had that al-Qaeda guy traveling through Kathmandu. When was that? 2012?"

"Before my time, sir," Ashra said. She hoped he would reveal the nature of this request soon, otherwise she might scream.

"Well, now they've requested assistance from the agent of ours that was involved in the Teller case as we call it nowadays. The entire thing with this mountain and the aliens." He sighed.

"They're an ancient progenitor species of mankind, not aliens," Ashra corrected.

"Anyway, they've requested, and we've granted them the request. You will be transferred to a secret site where they want to have your expertise on something. You'll be traveling in two hours. I assume you have your things packed?"

"That depends where I'm going," Ashra answered. "And what's requested of me."

"Well, pack your winter clothes. They've requested your presence in Antarctica."

"*Antarctica?*"

"Yes, my dear Agent Shah. Make us proud, will you? You're dismissed."

Ashra nodded and went for the door. Her mind was already on the assignment. Antarctica? What could possibly be in Antarctica?

****

Ashra knew she should have slept on the flight, but she was way too excited about the mysterious cooperation with the Americans. The plane from Kathmandu went to Dubai, and from there, a connecting flight brought her to South Africa. On a private airfield in the midst of the desert, she found a military transport awaiting her, guarded by unmarked American soldiers.

"Welcome to the madness!" A bearded man in civilian clothes greeted her. He wore baggy pants, a scarf, and flashy sunglasses. By the way he moved, Ashra knew right away she was talking to a soldier.

"Captain Miller. I'll be your escort for the rest of the trip. Enjoy the heat as long as you can."

The captain took her bag as Ashra climbed out of the jet and pointed to the large military transport plane resting on the airfield. Ashra took her own sunglasses from the pocket of her leather jacket.

"It looks like we won't be around for long. So, is this good timing, or did this plane come only for me?"

Captain Miller gave her a smile. "This is all for you. The real VIP treatment, ma'am." He grinned broadly and walked over to the transport. Another man came over and gave him his M5 assault rifle, which he put over his shoulder.

He hadn't asked for her name. His own name and rank could have been made up, too. This was the kind of operation that didn't exist. Executed from unmarked airfields, done by people without names. Had she been heading to any kind of populated area, she would have assumed this was a black operation; a covert intervention in a foreign country. Yet, who would one abduct or assassinate in Antarctica?

She followed Miller on board the large, empty transport plane and saw him stow away her bag. "I'll need the winter clothes in there before we land," Ashra said.

"Sure, we'll dress up when we pass Victoria."

"Where exactly are you bringing me?"

"The *exact* location is classified, but we'll fly to a site near the Concordia," the soldier said. Ashra wished she had studied the map of Antarctica more closely. "That's inland."

"I thought soldiers were forbidden in Antarctica? I never paid much attention to legal classes, but I feel like I remember that there is an international treaty forbidding any military presence in Antarctica?" Ashra said.

"Soldiers? There are no soldiers in Antarctica, ma'am. Only scientists, like you and me." The captain smiled.

"I see." Ashra couldn't help sneer. The man sat opposite her, his legs spread, his rifle between them. "Okay, do I get some of that scientific equipment, too?" Ashra pointed at the rifle.

"You won't need it. Nothing to shoot out there."

"What about ice bears?"

"Wrong pole. They're at the North Pole." Ashra had meant it as a joke. This guy wasn't big on humor, so she lost her motivation to try any further chatter. She wouldn't get anything out of him, but it seemed that he wanted something from her. American Special Forces were well trained.

"We've met before, you know?"

Ashra raised a brow. "We have?"

"Karachi." He nodded. "That facility you and your friend visited."

He was referring to the facility she and Elliot had been brought to as prisoners, where she'd arranged to be ambushed by the U.S. forces under the pretense it was a terrorist facility. It kind of was. That hardly qualified as being a "guest", as he put it.

"You were with the troops who did the clean sweep?" Ashra asked.

"Yes, ma'am. First on the ground back then. That was a bad one."

"So, Captain, compared to that, how do you think the thing you've got me into right now compares? Is it as bad?"

"Different kind of bad, I'd say. Nobody will be shooting at you, I suppose."

Ashra leaned back. The plane was making its way to the take-off position. She closed her eyes.

"You some sort of expert on this shit?" the captain asked.

Ashra almost smiled. So he *did* want something from her.

"What kind of shit would that be?" Ashra opened her eyes again.

"*Weird* stuff." He placed huge emphasis on the word "weird".

"I've had my share of weird stuff, I suppose," Ashra replied.

"Seems like you're an expert, as they made you an Alpha Asset. Usually those are brains. Scientists and programmers. Not Indian spies," the captain said.

"I'm from *Nepal*," she replied.

"Ah, sorry." He raised his hands in mock surrender. That hadn't been ignorance or lack of knowledge, he *genuinely* hadn't known where she came from; which meant her status was above his security clearance.

Someone considered her important.

****

The landing was surprisingly smooth. Ashra, now in her winter clothing of thermo-overalls and her red winter jacket, had looked out the window when they'd entered Antarctic airspace. Ice, mountains, and snow as far as the eye could see filled the landscape. As beautiful as the flat plains made of snow were, they lost their sensation after a while. As they prepared to land, she noticed they were close to an immense mountain range. Below them was a small base that looked like a group of red tin cans dug into the ice. A large antenna was visible next to one of them. The plane passed over and landed about half a mile closer to the mountains.

As soon as they touched down, the ramp in the back of the plane started lowering. Ashra zipped up her jacket as the ice-cold wind hissed into the plane.

"Welcome to Antarctica." The captain sighed. "This isn't a cold day, actually."

Ashra turned to him. "I'm used to the cold."

When the ramp reached the ground, Ashra saw a lone man stepping through the snow toward the plane. He took off his goggles and hood; revealing a blond, blue-eyed man, who was smiling at her. She assumed he was the welcome committee.

"Ms. Shah. I'm Boyd Green. Welcome to Antarctica!" the man yelled over the dying down engines of the plane. Ashra stepped out and offered her hand.

"Ashra Shah, Nepalese Bureau of Investigations, pleased to meet you." He took her hand. The captain stepped out of the plane and was greeted with only a nod. He nodded back. So Green wasn't part of the military chain of command, or he would have saluted. "I guess you're with the CIA?"

"Yes." Green laughed. "I'm with the CIA. We're very grateful you could make room in your schedule on such short notice."

"Not a problem, believe me." Ashra smiled.

"Call me Boyd. So, I guess you want to settle in before going to work?"

"Ashra. Well, Boyd, to be honest I would love to know why the hell I've been dragged here. Nobody briefed me on anything. I've received no orders from my own people."

"No, of course not. We couldn't share anything about the nature of this site or mission. So, if you don't mind after the long and certainly exhausting journey, I'll show you. Probably the easiest way to explain this." Boyd gestured to the ice fields toward the mountains.

"Sure," Ashra said.

"Good. Captain, get her stuff to the base. Ashra and I will have a little walk," Boyd said, beginning to walk. "It's not far."

"I don't mind walking through snow."

"Right. You're an expert in mountain climbing, snowy environments, and operating in the cold. I read that on your file. Was an interesting read."

"So why don't you tell me what this is about?"

"This is a cold day, you know? A few months back you could have run around here in a bikini." Ashra laughed. "Not a joke. Twenty-five degrees Celsius as our Danish colleagues put it. Seventy-seven Fahrenheit. In Antarctica. Talk about climate change being a lie, hmm?"

"Yeah, we have the same problem. Melting glaciers are endangering entire regions in my country." Ashra wondered where this conversation was going.

"Well, then you know the problem. Here in Antarctica, there's a *million* years of ice that's started melting. Every forty hours a billion metric tons of ice becomes water. Poses a challenge to the scientists here. Also, this creates an opportunity. There are parts of ice now reachable that have been buried under tons of ice and snow for centuries. These mountains lost twenty-five percent of their glaciers. One was especially volatile. When the ice grew too thin, it broke into two parts, and the northern one collapsed. Quite a spectacle, I was told. I only saw the videos, but I'm sure that wasn't the same." Boyd was slow in the snow. He was obviously not used to this environment. They were now approaching a large cliff. Possibly the place where the glacier had collapsed.

"So what does that have to do with me? I'm an expert in black markets and such things. I've tracked illegal smuggling operations for the last six months. I guess this isn't a problem here, is it?" Ashra asked.

"No, except a few bottles of whiskey, we're fine on that front. Well, you also happen to be good at finding people, which was why you helped find a man named Professor Teller about seven months ago. You *did* find him, and with him, according to your report, you found quite a unique construct. A city within a mountain. Ancient, yet quite intact, right?" Ashra swallowed and nodded. Boyd made a gesture toward the nearby cliff. Ashra drew her jacket tighter around herself and slowly stepped forward. When she saw what was below, in the giant rift in the ice, her jaw dropped. Boyd stood next to her and smiled.

"Yeah," he said. "We all felt like that when we first saw it. So, what do you say, Ashra?" He looked at her, and Ashra regained her composure. She slowly turned her eyes to the American CIA agent. She had only one thing to say. One thing she knew right away, they had to do now.

"Get Professor Elliot Brand."

Chapter 2

"The civilization which I have dubbed the Ancients is real. I have seen proof. Teller and I have been in that city, deep under the Himalaya. You all have my report in front of you. I know I've no evidence to present today of what we found back then, but I'm willing to put my reputation at risk here to continue my work, and I can only say that I believe this to be the greatest archeological finding in the history of humanity. Not following up on it, not going after what we now know is a truth that contradicts everything we believe in, would be a mistake." Elliot Brand folded his hands as he stood before the twelve men in front of him. The Funding Circle was allocating the institute's research money, and he had applied for a good chunk of it to gather the necessary resources to continue his research.

The twelve men were all distinguished senior members of the scientific community. Wearing traditional three-piece suits and sipping tea, some occasionally went through his paper; some seemed simply bored.

"Professor Brand, you're a man who has the reputation of being reasonable and mindful. The pride of our faculty and a rising star in the world of archeology. Your work on the verge of technology and how our scientific methods can be enriched by it has been . . . enlightening. Visionary, some might even say. The only stain on your resume has been that of your mentor, the late Professor Dr. Teller, who once was a respected expert in his field before turning to more obscure theories over time, gaining popularity while leaving the path of real scientific research." This was Paul Lennox, the youngest member of the committee, barely ten years older than Elliot. Elliot cleared his throat.

"He was unorthodox, and nobody disdains his public comments and the majority of his theories more than I. But what I'm reporting here is that he has been right. About the existence of a civilization that preceded ours, that lived a million years ago, whose traces have all but vanished as time has washed them away. He was right, and he found it, hidden away under the mountains of Nepal."

"There is no proof you can present to us here today," Lennox said with a sigh.

"Most of the evidence has been destroyed, I admit. A loss for our craft that I regret deeply. Yet, I have presented the platinum tablets with the language of the Ancients. I have shown the committee the analysis of London's finest laboratory, that has confirmed both their age and unique composition. You also have my word that I encountered this mystery first-hand and spent days in that lost city under the mountain. I barely made it out alive, and Professor Teller, who you think so lowly about, didn't make it. He's buried down there under the mountain, having died for what he believed in." Elliot saw Lennox wasn't convinced.

"The composition of those tablets indicates a much younger origin than what the dating implied, so we can't rule out they have been faked by Professor Teller himself and presented to you as proof," Lennox said.

"The dating has been triple checked. I don't think it can be questioned." Elliot had to resist hammering his fist on the desk.

"Well, the tablets might be old, but that doesn't mean the signs on it are," Lennox said. Elliot had to fight down his growing anger. Lennox was about to say something else, but Professor Davis, the head of the institute, raised his hand and silenced him. The old man still held an authority in the circle few men could match.

16

"Elliot. Professor Brand," he began. "Your achievements are above question, as is your reputation. Yet you come before us with very little to offer. The tablets notwithstanding, there is *no* proof of the city itself. Not even a cell phone picture or a video. The tragedy that happened in those mountains has left you without a witness, too." He gave a deep sigh.

"What if I have a witness?" Elliot asked. "A member of the Nepali intelligence community who was there too. A reasonable young woman, not in any way associated with Teller or me before—"

"Are you talking about the same Nepali women you were romantically involved with over the summer?"

How did he know? How the hell could he possibly know about such a private matter?

"Professor Brand." Davis said. "I suggest you find proof of your claims—scientific, reliable, undeniable proof—and we'll review your application again. Until then, I would advise to withdraw it, to protect your reputation and spare you the public humiliation of failing with it."

Elliot looked at the old man. He understood what he said. They would say no, so all he could do was protect himself from the humiliation. They needed proof, and he wanted the money to actually *get* proof.

Nodding in silent consent, he didn't say another word, instead leaned back and looked at Lennox, as the circle proceeded to the next point.

****

17

"I can see in your face that it didn't go well," Abas said, as Elliot entered the office before hurling his suitcase against the wall. "Also, there are other indicators."

Elliot turned to him and sighed. "It was a full-blown disaster. They made me withdraw the whole submission, then kicked me out a few minutes later. That bastard Lennox, he wanted to sabotage me! He came prepared. He knew about Ashra. How the hell . . ." Elliot stopped as the small Afghan with his large brown eyes handed him a tea.

"Calm down. You'll find another source of funding," Abas said.

"Abas, you've never been in university. If the committee says no, that *means* no. Nobody else will even touch me. Had they given me half the budget, or even a quarter, I could have shopped the project around. Asked for funds and submitted for extra money." Elliot shook his head and sipped the tea. It was delicious. He looked up at his friend and smiled.

"This your special one?"

"Found a shop run by an Afghan family who still seem to have an open line to my home country. They have all kinds of local specialties, even from my home region." Abas smiled back.

"Yes, there's little you don't find in London. It's a big city," Elliot said, barely paying attention anymore.

"There's someone asking for you."

"Not now, Abas." He circled around his desk, that was now covered with articles and books he had studied. "I need to read those nonsense reports about the Moricoxi." Elliot rubbed his forehead. "The Bigfoot of South America—tall, smart, and living in the most obscure and unexplored parts of . . . ah, damn. I feel like

18

one of those nutjobs!" Elliot looked at Abas; the man couldn't have cared less.

"Listen, Elliot, you know I've no idea what you're talking about there. I appreciate you gave me this job, but maybe . . . One of your students . . ."

"Abas, you led my dig in Askalan. You were closer to ancient ruins and artifacts than any of those, and you did a marvelous job preserving them. Don't make yourself smaller than you are."

"I'm good with my hands. But I'm not good with my brain, Elliot. I'm not smart. Not like everybody else around here," Abas said. "I can barely read your language!"

"You've learned a lot, made progress. Be patient. And by the way, *I* decide who I hire and who I don't hire." Elliot leaned back. He owed the man his life, but more than that—he trusted him. How many people could he trust? Now that he was a lunatic looking for an ancient civilization . . . probably few.

"Okay," Abas said.

"Ecuador. I think I want to go to Ecuador first, if we ever get funding."

"Why Ecuador?"

"The Lost City of Giants. Those Ancients, when I found their city and that skeleton, they were all taller than humans. In Ecuador, they discovered ruins from a city in 2012 that was built in a strange way. They seemed oversized. Not only oversized by the standard of humans back then who were considerably smaller than us, but even by our standards. As if the inhabitants had been well above two meters. The age of the ruins is all wrong—much too young. But maybe those were descendants of the Ancients.

Leftovers, that bred with humans. I don't know. It's the best I have."

"Elliot," he said gently, "I really think you should talk to that woman... It seemed important."

Elliot held his gaze, then nodded in agreement. He was too distracted for work anyway. "I have a lecture to do. If it's important, she'll come back."

****

He entered the auditorium five minutes early, as always. It was filled with students; his lectures were always popular. He beheld his students, then smiled. It was surreal that he now had to talk about laser mapping. It felt like a waste of time. Yet, these were the archeologists of tomorrow, and he had accepted the duty to educate them.

"Hello, everybody. I must say, I feel honored that so many of you have shown up, while all my colleagues complain about drying up streams of students now that the holidays are at the doors." A laughter rippled through the ranks.

"So, today we'll talk about the last and final method of use of modern technology in the field of archeology. It's called LIDAR, sometimes spelled with a small i, or even LADAR. It's commonly known as "laser mapping", and it's a powerful tool—a powerful tool we use to map objects, even rooms and entire complexes, and make exact digital copies of them for research purposes, archiving, and analysis. It's a method for determining ranges and variable distances by targeting an object with a laser and measuring the time for the reflected light to return to the receiver. It's a powerful tool that allows for detailed, high-resolution maps to be made with precision and at a speed that was unthinkable before. I present you a case study now, that I have personally overseen. It's a tomb at Askalan that I mapped last year. We were only able to map seventy-percent of the complex, but I think you'll see how powerful this method can be." He took the remote control and dimmed the light. He pressed play, and the video one of his assistants had prepared appeared. Elliot withdrew to the side of the auditorium and leaned against the doorframe. He watched the students, as they all seemed absorbed by the film. His eyes went through the ranks. Faces were hard to make out in the dim light. Sometimes, lighter pictures illuminated the auditorium, and he saw some of them typing messages on their cell phones and some making notes— they obviously didn't know the entire script was available online.

He was approaching the age when he began missing his twenties. The hardships had slowly faded into the oblivion of forgetfulness, and what remained had been the feeling of freedom he recalled. He thought about how complicated everything had felt then, and how *un*complicated it truly was, compared to later life.

He let his view wander over those assembled, and just as he was about to turn to his laptop, he saw her. She sat in the seventh row, smiling at him as their gaze met. Ashra Shah; wearing a leather jacket and looking right at him. He felt his heart skip a beat. The smile he returned had a short lifespan, as he realized what this meant. She had been in Nepal the last time she had contacted him; it had been a while. He assumed that had been her way to deal with what had been a silent break up; the acknowledgment that a relationship between London and Kathmandu was impossible. Yet now, she was sitting there serenely, and she hadn't even announced herself. She hadn't called or written a message. So she wasn't here as a tourist, or even to see him. She couldn't announce her arrival because *it was secret*. She was here on official business.

21

"So, can anyone tell me what you just saw?"

He felt he needed all of his concentration to even stand through the rest of the lecture.

****

"Hey." She grinned as she approached him, while the students streamed out of the auditorium. In her outfit, she looked totally normal around here. Her Nepali origins were nothing special in a multi-cultural city like London.

"Hey, Ashra. Good to see you." He tried to hide his excitement at seeing her again. He had missed her. Not a day had passed where he hadn't regretted that day in Karachi when they had parted ways. "How long have you been in London?"

"An hour. I came right for you after I landed."

"Obviously you skipped the customs controls," he said, as he put his laptop into his leather bag. She looked down with that bashful look whenever he caught her out with something. Adorable, but now used against him. "Guess the advantages of a private jet." He checked his watch.

"Courtesy of the British Government," Ashra said, still looking at the ground. "Listen . . ."

"Wait. Before you say anything . . ." Elliot sighed. He wanted to kiss her, but he knew that was no longer appropriate "How are you?"

Ashra laughed. "I'm good, Elliot. I'm good. But I'm not here . . . to see you. I mean I *am* here to see you, but . . ." Ashra trailed off, and he saw how stupid she must have felt.

"Official business," Elliot said. "You could have called."

"Where I need to bring you . . . I wasn't sure if a call would be enough," Ashra replied cryptically.

"Ashra, one call from you and I would go anywhere." Elliot stepped closer to her. "You should know that."

"Good to hear. We've already talked to the dean, and you'll be free of all duties until further notice. He'll take over your lectures," Ashra said.

"Ashra, where are we going?" Elliot asked; she seemed so terribly serious all of a sudden. "And who is this *we* you're talking about?"

Ashra looked aside, and Elliot saw they were no longer alone. A man in a black suit stood there, and next to him, a young woman in uniform. He wasn't good with military stuff, but he was pretty sure it was an American one—the little flag on her arm kind of gave her away. She was short for a soldier, in her twenties, and her face looked serious as she stood with her hands behind her back, her body tense.

"This is Sgt. McKenzie of the United States Army. She'll organize your transportation," Ashra said. "And Mr. Smith here is with MI6 and will give you a speech on secrecy and your security clearing. The British Government was kind enough to help us with arranging your implementation into the mission."

"Transportation where?" Elliot asked with a sharp laugh. He felt like he was in a bad spy movie.

"Antarctica," Ashra replied. "I can't tell you a lot, but . . . we found something there. Something you need to see."

Elliot suddenly understood. The Ancients. They were here because with Teller dead, he was the foremost expert on the mysterious progenitor species called the Ancients.

23

Chapter 3

Ashra watched Elliot standing on the cliff and looking down into the rift below. They had flown separately, which she regretted. After Elliot had a moment to appreciate setting foot on the last continent he had never visited, he had insisted on seeing why he had been brought here in the first place.

Boyd Green had walked him to the cliff and given almost the exact same speech about melting ice he had given to her. Then Elliot had arrived at the giant trench, and wasn't as surprised as she had been. Of course not. He had already figured out why he was here. If Elliot Brand was anything, it was smart. He just stood there in silence and stared at what the collapsed ice had revealed. The large structures were shimmering through the ice, and at some points they were breaking through it. Smooth, white-stone pillars rose up. Giant arches were spread out for yards down below; a colossal dish made of stone was also visible—easily three-hundred-feet from one side to the other.

"So? What do you say, Professor?" Boyd asked.

"This is astounding," Elliot replied and looked at Ashra. "When did you find it?"

"Eight days ago. Must have been here for months without anybody stumbling over it. A group of climate scientists came across it while investigating the collapsed glacier."

Elliot turned to Ashra. "They got you here?"

"We needed an expert from the intelligence community and found her. So we requested her help. She implied we would need your expertise to get a proper evaluation of what we're dealing with," Boyd explained.

"This is . . . a military operation?" Elliot looked at McKenzie and Miller, who stood close by.

"Yes, it's a classified military operation."

"This should be run by scientists. I mean, this is . . . this is probably the greatest find in *human history*. This is proof, *undeniable* proof of the existence of a civilization long before the first humans even built a house of mud and stones."

"How old do you estimate those ruins are?"

"I'm not a geologist. But I'd say this wasn't built in a frozen environment. Look at the structure. It has openings everywhere. Nothing to indicate the creators needed to keep the cold out. About thirty-million years ago, a dramatic shift in climate happened somewhere between the Eocene and Oligocene epochs. The South Pole was frozen for much longer, but as newer studies show, this here was actually land covered by a large rainforest. A very stable, tropical climate, unchanged since the extinction of the dinosaurs. Then it became dramatically colder, slowly changing the Antarctica into the icy place we know today," Elliot continued. "Even if we assume this was built when the region was already cooling off, we're talking about *millions* of years. Long before humanity came into existence."

"How many millions of years?" Boyd asked. Elliot looked at Ashra, then at the CIA agent.

"Twenty at least. Maybe even more," Elliot said, shaking his head in disbelief.

"How long before humanity would that be?" Ashra asked, feeling she hadn't understood the full gravity of what she had

26

considered an already spectacular finding. She had assumed this was another ruin of the Ancients. But what Elliot now implied was . . . unthinkable.

"The first hominids appeared four million years ago. The oldest fossils of upright walking apes were found in Ethiopia. So even if we assume that we haven't found any older ones and we're doubling that age, which is unlikely, the earliest predecessors of humanity wouldn't be even close to the age of this place."

"But this is the Ancients, right? This is their site. They must have been much older than Teller thought?" Ashra said.

Elliot shook his head. "It's too early to say, but it isn't the same Ancients we found. Look at the architecture. The ruins we found in Nepal were cuboidal with clear angles. This structure is based on curves, and we can see signs of erosion. The Himalayan ruins mysteriously didn't erode. I'm not sure we're looking at the same species. If anything, I would work on the hypothesis that whoever built this was truly the ancestor of the Ancients. A species much older." Elliot turned back to the ruins. "There are entries. Down there is something that actually looks like a gate of sorts." He pointed to the bottom of the rift. "Did you enter it?"

"Not yet," Boyd answered. "But there's something I need to show you. Something that will make it clear why this has to be a military operation." The American turned. "Let's go to the base. I think you'll find what I have to show you very interesting." He began to walk. Elliot threw Ashra a look, but all she could do was shrug. The American hadn't shared anything with her yet, as she had left straight away to get Elliot. She was glad he was here. Obviously, he would be invaluable to their mission. That wasn't the only reason though. The truth was, she was happy because the mission gave her an excuse to be near him.

"I missed you," Ashra couldn't help say, as soon as Boyd was far away enough not to hear them.

Elliot turned away from the ruins and gave her a smile. "I missed you too, Ashra." Ashra returned the smile and went to follow Boyd. As much as she would have loved to talk now, she knew it would have to wait. They weren't here to rekindle their relationship. This was way more important than any of that. What was down there, revealed by the melting ice, had the potential to change everything. Even she understood that.

****

They entered the largest of the four buildings that together were called Outpost 41. Inside, there were rooms on either side. Voices were heard from behind, and a few soldiers in full snow gear passed them as they entered. They saluted to Miller and McKenzie, but Ashra could see in their eyes who they really respected—Boyd Green. He was obviously the man calling the shots.

"Follow me to my office," Boyd said, leading the way. Ashra had been here already, but saw Elliot reading the labels next to the doors. Living Room, Comms, Labs, Computer Pool, Storage, Kitchen. Outpost 41 was fully equipped to outlast several winters without restocking or support. That wasn't surprising considering it was almost six hours away from the next outpost, if one used the helicopter that parked outside.

Boyd took a sharp turn, and entered what he called his office. Long tables that indicated it was actually meant to be a lab, were in the center. Empty fridges for ice probes not plugged into the station generator, sat silently against the walls. A few bags he had put in the corner barely seemed to have been touched. The only real piece of equipment he had, was a laptop sitting on the front desk. He stepped behind the desk and typed something into the laptop; his password, Ashra assumed. Her training forced her to recognize it had sixteen digits—and therefore would be very hard to crack.

"What I'm about to tell you is highly classified. *Top secret*. You aren't allowed to ever discuss it with anybody outside this room. You understand?"

Ashra and Elliot both nodded. Elliot stepped forward and looked around. More used to scientific stations like this, Ashra wondered what he was seeing.

"We developed a satellite system a few years back codenamed the Newton. It's able to detect electromagnetic fields from an orbit around Earth," Boyd said.

"Guess that one comes in handy when you want to distinguish fake nuclear tests from real ones or know who actually has a bomb and who doesn't," Elliot said. "Nukes produce electromagnetic pulses, right?"

"Exactly. North Korea, Iran. Newton gives us a clearer picture what's going on there. Also, some countries have the desire to acquire nuclear technology. That isn't our problem today." Boyd said, his face illuminated by the laptop screen. "Anyway, Newton passed this site a few days ago, and with some convincing from our side, it took a few shots. This is what came out." Boyd turned the laptop around, a geological map in white and gray showing the area and the mountains nearby. In its center, was a large red sphere.

"This is the rift," Boyd explained, pointing with his finger at the red spot, then drawing a line that contained some gray areas.

"And that red sphere there . . . is an electromagnetic field?" Elliot asked in disbelief.

29

Ashra moved next to him and leaned forward. "How big is that?" she asked, estimating it to be several hundred feet in her own head.

"About right. It's an electromagnetic field. It seems to have its origin in the center of the ruins. See . . ." Boyd leaned over the laptop screen and pressed a button. Another map appeared with red and blue areas. "The blue indicates the extent of the ruins."

Elliot leaned forward. "That is a whole bloody city!" He gasped and looked at Boyd.

"About the size of Austin, Texas. Yes." Boyd nodded. "From the outline, I'd say it looks more like a giant reactor or something. Circles getting smaller and smaller, like perimeters. This field is right at the center of it. You understand what an electromagnetic field needs? To be constantly upheld, it needs energy. Indicating that in these ruins, is an energy source. A considerable one. This field has an intensity of a fifty-megaton nuclear explosion."

"Do bombs that big even exist?" Ashra shuddered. She had never heard of any such devastating weapon.

"No, not even close to it. My guys from tech actually say no energy source known to mankind could possibly create a field like that," Boyd said.

"That's impossible," Elliot said. "These ruins are millions of years old. No nuclear reaction would last this long. No generator, reactor, or power plant could still be working after this time!"

"Which is why I asked about the age. Whatever this is, it isn't anything we're familiar with. An energy source seemingly unlimited and unaffected by any timespan," Boyd said.

"You think it's a weapon?" Ashra asked Boyd.

"Yes. That's exactly what we think. What else needs such excessive amounts of energy?"

"Well, if this civilization was further developed than ours, how could we know? They might have used technology beyond our scope of understanding. Tech that needs such an amount of energy."

"I hope so. I want you to find out. That's why you two are here. To tell me what this is and if it poses a danger to us." Boyd said.

"It makes no sense." Elliot folded his arms. Ashra saw he was thinking. His face almost revealed the multitude of thoughts rushing through his mind.

"What makes no sense?" Boyd asked.

"Keeping an energy source like this active. The ruins are unpopulated, so either they were abandoned, or the creators died out. In either event, there was a crisis, leaving the place abandoned. An energy source of this power is dangerous. It can't be left unchecked. Anyone with the intellect able to build it would deactivate it," Elliot said.

"Except it can't be deactivated," Ashra vocalized her thoughts; Elliot stared at her. "Sorry, just thinking."

"No, you're right. Maybe it can't be switched off. Either it served a function that needed to be fulfilled after the creators left, or it can't be deactivated by design. An eternal energy source. Possibly inaccessible or simply producing so much power nobody can get near it. Yet, it seems to produce heat."

"What makes you think so?" Boyd asked.

"The ruins. They seem to be hollow. After millions of years, they should be filled with ice and snow. Something kept the cold out. The climate in there might be surprisingly warm."

"We've located no heat signature."

"A few degrees would be enough. Nothing that shows on thermal scans or stands out," Elliot said.

"This is your area of expertise. We got everything you need, and what we don't have we can get here within a day. What's our first step?"

"We need to enter the ruins. I need some of my equipment from London."

"We'll get you that. But . . . one step at a time. First, I want you to meet our scientists."

"So you have scientists here after all?" Elliot smirked.

"Of course we do. We were just missing a professor of archeology," Boyd replied.

****

The living room—as the general cantina, meeting area, and recreational area was called—was one large room. It contained a billiard table, a chess set, a TV, and a fridge that seemed to hold mostly sweets. It also had long tables to eat at, comfortable chairs with Bluetooth connected headphones on them, and a large assortment of DVDs. Inside stood a number of soldiers, all wearing the white winter jackets and assault rifles on their back; none of them had anything on them assigning their ranks or even indicated which army they belonged to. The foremost of the men, tall, handsome and blond with striking blue eyes, smiled at Ashra as she entered. Except for McKenzie, these men had probably not seen a woman for a while. Ashra returned the smile, but stepped a bit closer to Elliot.

Those soldiers weren't the only ones there; there were the three specs. She called them that because all three were wearing glasses; from the way they moved, looked, and spoke, she had needed less than a minute to understand they weren't soldiers, but actually scientists. The eldest stood up; he ignored the soldiers completely and approached Elliot. He wiped his hand on his laboratory coat, which looked so incongruous in Antarctica, then he offered it to Elliot.

"Professor Elliot Brand, we heard you would be coming. I'm Dr. Rubin Gernsbeck. I'm what you could call the head of our small science department here." He gave a modest chuckle. Elliot, always polite yet focused and straight to the point, shook the man's hand.

"Thank you, Dr. Gernsbeck. What's your field if I may ask?"

"Geophysics, specialized in glaciology. I led the research that stumbled upon this . . . mess."

"And you've been here since then?" Elliot looked at Boyd.

"I understand the gravity of the matter and volunteered to stay here for the sake of safety, secrecy, and to ensure this was scientifically handled properly," Dr. Gernsbeck said.

Ashra realized that Elliot had picked something up she had missed. Something about Dr Gernsbeck's answer had made Elliot hesitate for a moment. Elliot turned to the other two people; Ashra saw the soldiers exchange irritated glances for being ignored. They clearly felt they were running the show and not given the respect they deserved by the incoming professor.

The second bespectacled man; red-haired and overweight with a gray turtleneck, pushed himself up and greeted Elliot. "Hey. Jonah Gustavsson. I'm the weather specialist."

"Speaking of which, how's the prediction for the cold front?" Boyd asked.

"Whiteout in 26," Gustavsson said.

"You're military?" Ashra blinked.

"Danish pioneer, ma'am. My government lent me to this mission as there was nobody else available on such short notice."

"Whiteout is a snowstorm, right?" Elliot asked.

"Yes, one so intense you basically have zero sight, only white. Whiteout. We have a stormfront approaching from the coast. Should reach Concordia in a day, and it'll be here two hours later," Gustavsson said.

The final man, the one who didn't fit in, stood up; his hands remained in his pockets. He threw Boyd an almost bored look. He was young, maybe even younger than Ashra, with jet black hair.

"Justin Pressman. I'm IT," he said. "Pleasure to meet you."

"IT?" Elliot asked in surprise. "You expect any compounder problems in a million-year-old ruin?"

Justin laughed. "Professor Brand, Elliot Brand. You wrote that paper on the MRADs, didn't you?"

"Mobile Research Application Drones? God, that paper is ancient. My first steps into the common ground archeology has with technology. I'm surprised you even know it," Elliot replied.

"Are you kidding me? I worked on that project for three years!" Justin said.

"Wait. What? The whole system was a theoretical study. It would cost easily ten million to produce a prototype," Elliot said.

"Ten? Oh no, it cost us almost twenty-two," Justin said with a nonchalant shrug.

"You *built* them?" Elliot asked.

"When we had the Tora Bora disaster, the military looked for technological solutions to the problems with those maze-like caves. Turned out you had the right idea. Just not a good scope of what it could be used for." Justin said.

"Wait, that must be some kind of patent infringement!" Elliot looked at Boyd.

"Ah, Professor, these guys usually wave around some docs signed by big wigs from DC, then mumble something about national security, and those problems simply go away in my experience," Justin answered.

Boyd laughed. "If you solve me this riddle, I'll be your crown witness in the lawsuit, Professor. Someone at Langley thought you might find the drones useful though, so we have them there with us just in case you need them."

Elliot seemed to decide to leave it at that. "Do you guys know Ashra Shah? She's my . . . a friend. She has experience crawling through ruins," Elliot said; all three men nodded at her.

"Well, what do you think about the thermomagnetic energy source?" Gernsbeck asked directly.

"I think I would love to hear your thoughts on it. I only arrived half an hour ago. You must have developed a theory on it," Elliot said.

"Maybe you start work later. I want to introduce you to Private William Pierce first," Boyd gestured to the blond man. "Private Pierce, this is Professor Brand and Agent Shah. You'll be responsible for their security while they remain with us," Boyd said.

"Yes, sir." The man said. "Professor? Agent Shah?" He gave both a nod.

"I doubt we need security, Mr. Green," Elliot said to Boyd. "Or do we expect anybody to shoot at us?"

"Did we ever expect?" Ashra said. "Happened anyway. Didn't it?"

Elliot looked at her, then Pierce. "Point taken. Private? I'm simply Elliot."

"My pleasure, Professor. I won't get in your way, I promise," Pierce said.

"So do we have anywhere we can discuss what we found here?" Elliot asked.

"The lab," Gernsbeck said.

"Boyd, how many soldiers do you have here?" Ashra asked.

"Twenty-five. Two shifts each," Boyd said. "These three fellas here and you two, as well as Mitchell, the helicopter pilot, and myself—we're exactly thirty-one people out here."

"Thanks." Ashra looked at the present soldiers.

"Are you coming?" Elliot asked. Ashra realized she was invited to go along with the science team. With a smile, she followed.

"Anything wrong?" Elliot asked her as they left the room.

"I don't understand the logic of the mission. Twenty-five soldiers aren't enough to defend the ruins against any sort of serious attack. Also, they don't guard the ruins but the buildings. I think there's something Boyd isn't telling us yet," she whispered. Elliot glanced back at Boyd, who was now talking with the soldiers. Pierce followed them, and Elliot couldn't press any further, but in his eyes, Ashra saw that he understood. Those men were guarding something—and it was in *this* base, not out there.

Chapter 4

Elliot wished Teller could be here. He would probably dive into this. He would develop ideas, and compare them to obscure theories—that shockingly would turn out to be right, no matter how ridiculous his assumptions sounded in the beginning. Teller had died in some other ruins, though. Ruins like these; yet so very different.

They entered the laboratory, a room not unlike Boyd's bureau, but the fridges were filled with large cylinders that showed ice samples. Microscopes and laptops filled the long table which had chairs around it. There were white boards, on which numbers had been scribbled. Elliot scanned them as he entered. They had calculated the age of this thing.

"Nineteen million years?" Elliot asked.

"A rough estimate based on the ice layers around it. Yes. Twenty million years," Gernsbeck said.

"Well, may I start with the elephant in the room?" Justin asked. "Do you think those things are real, Professor?"

Elliot had to smirk. One skeptical mind was always good. It balanced those with too much fantasy.

"From the size and appearance, I would say if this was a forgery it must have taken centuries to prepare it. No way to be sure until we have analyzed and dated samples, but yes, I believe this to be a twenty-million-year-old ruin," Elliot said.

"Just out of interest, how old is the oldest human ruins that have been dug up?" Justin asked.

"Adam's calendar in South Africa is probably 300,000 years old," Elliot answered. "Buildings? Jericho. Palestine territories. We found remains there dating back 11,000 years. I personally encountered a ruin I estimated to be a million years old under the Himalaya. Ashra was there, too," he added.

"So this is twenty-two times older? Basically, pre-human ruins? Is that even possible?" Ashra asked, joining the skeptical Justin.

"Well, I think I explained to you before, but for the rest of you . . . yes, it is. Truth is, we can't rule out the existence of anything beyond half a million years ago. A few years back, there was a paper that actually found great recognition in my professional circles. It was based on the idea there might have been highly developed civilizations before ours. How, you ask? Quite simple. Another scientific work, one you might have heard about—the Population Zero study? What would happen if your population dropped to zero over night? Well, all we built and created would collapse, dissolve, or erode within ten thousand years. After a hundred thousand years, only a few structures, isotopes, and plastics would remain as proof of our existence. Half a million years and nothing, nothing at all would remain that proves that our civilization existed. Radioactive waste will be gone. Any concrete will be dust, any metal too. Plastic will have dissolved. Even titanium will have eroded. There would be no sign of mankind at all." Elliot leaned against the table. He knew Ashra had heard all of this before.

"In other words, a bunch of civilizations could have existed and vanished, and we wouldn't even know?" Gustavsson said.

"Well, that could be the case, yes." Elliot nodded.

40

"You an expert on those?" Justin asked. "Thought you're a tech guy?"

"Well, Ashra and I and my former mentor, Professor Teller, actually found a potential . . . we found signs that such a civilization might have existed a million years ago," Elliot said. "Which made me an expert worth getting here, I guess."

"We found ruins, ancient ruins," Ashra added.

"Why have I never heard of them?" Justin folded his arms.

"We couldn't secure evidence, and I'm still working on my paper on the findings," Elliot replied. Ashra gave him a surprised look. She knew how long he had been working on that paper. She probably guessed the same thing that he had slowly come to understand—he might never publish it. Without proof, it would be endangering his entire career.

"There would be fossils, right?" Justin said. "Ah, we would have found fossils if there was any proto-human species running around!" Justin seemed proud to have found a flaw in Elliot's theory. He knew the type. They considered themselves so smart. Smarter than anyone else.

"Yes, indeed. Fossils would be a possibility." Elliot said.

"Yet, we found none!" Justin raised his voice.

"Didn't we?" Elliot said. The men now all looked at him. "We find bones every day we can't categorize. Incomplete skeletons and so on. Without knowing what they are, they're usually not even collected. Thrown away or stored in some warehouse in case someone finds a fitting counterpart or something. Basically, they are forgotten. So maybe we found fossils of them. If they left any. Maybe their burial rights included burning, maybe they put them all into one place, where we've never found them. In our case, here the answer is more obvious, of course."

"How could we find the remains of an Antarctica-based civilization or any fossils when it was all buried under millions of tons of ice?" Gernsbeck said.

"Exactly." Elliot nodded.

"So you think that humanity didn't develop a hundred thousand years ago, but actually more like twenty-two million years? And we never found a human skeleton that old?" Justin was shaking his head.

"Who said anything about human skeletons?" Elliot asked.

Justin let out a scathing laugh. "Wait, what are you telling us? These were aliens?"

"No, not at all. I'm just saying . . ." Elliot began. "I sound like my old mentor now, and I always despised it when he put wild theories like this out there, but . . . listen guys, I'm thinking on my feet, okay? Three hours ago, I didn't even know these ruins existed. Twenty-two million years old, that is more than a game changer. This is rewriting history books from chapter one." Elliot dragged a hand down his face, finding it hard even to answer the question.

"More like writing a prequel to the history books, isn't it?" Gustavsson joked.

"Prelude to humanity, not a bad title!" Justin agreed.

"What is it you wanted to say? About not being human?" Ashra asked; she wasn't so easily distracted. Always a quick thinker, always aware when he tried to dodge the question.

"Twenty-two million years, nineteen million years. It makes no difference. Humanity wasn't around back then. Not even the slightest sign of upright walking apes," Elliot said. "So why would we assume . . ."

As he looked around, he saw all of them were staring at him now.

"What you mean is this civilization might have been *non-human*? Like, something else other than human?" Gernsbeck asked.

"What I'm saying is, that from what we know about humanity, what we know about their official development, and even if we take the more radical ideas and concepts into consideration as absolute truth . . . it's actually not very likely we'll find a twenty-two-million-year-old species that is connected to humanity. We developed from apes. They learned to walk upright, their brains developed, and they started using tools. Actually, we found evidence another ancient species might have had a hand in all of that. A million years ago that might have happened. But what are the chances apes developed twice in that direction? I mean, were there even apes in Antarctica?" Elliot shrugged.

"I think that's a bit farfetched," Gernsbeck said.

"As I'm thinking about it, you have pictures of the ruins?" Elliot asked. "There's sort of an entrance . . ."

"Yes, we have that one," Justin said. He leaned over a table and got his laptop. He opened a program, then turned it to Elliot, showing the large entrance that looked like a slide in the walls.

"See, this thing is what? Nine-feet high? Twelve maybe?" Elliot asked.

"Roundabout, yeah," Justin said.

43

"Why is it so narrow? Can't be more than a couple of feet long. three maybe? Four?" Elliot guessed. "Barely broad enough for a human to step through."

"Could have been their aesthetic style, or maybe it was serving a purpose. Easier to defend," Gernsbeck threw back.

"Agreed," Elliot said. "We don't know anything about the inhabitants of these ruins. Nothing at all. It'll take years before we ever learn enough to have a clear picture. We're pioneers here. Each and every one of us. Not the dream team of archeology when it comes to our qualifications, but we're all there is for now. So all we can do is build one hypothesis after another, then try to prove them." Elliot looked at the men. "My hypothesis is, that door wasn't made by a mind that resembles a human one. Let's see if that turns out to be true."

"Of course," Gernsbeck said. Elliot saw the men had doubts. Doubts were good. He needed someone to control his line of thinking. Otherwise, he would get lost in his own theories.

"The electromagnetic signature, you said you have a theory on it?" Elliot asked.

"A *theory* is a large word. We did scans of the ruins, and Mr. Green gave us access to both the original scan of the area and the newer one made today," Gernsbeck said. Elliot hadn't known they had done two scans.

"And?" Elliot asked.

"Well, we've also scanned the ruins using echolocation tools. They weren't designed for such scans, but we know roughly the size of these ruins. And they're massive. Also, no movement inside as far as we can tell," Gernsbeck explained.

"What did the scans reveal about the energy source?" Elliot asked.

"It's growing," Gernsbeck said. "At a rate of 1.38% per day."

He let the words sink in; Elliot needed a moment to digest what he had just been told. Then a thought occurred to him, "Wait, how long ago would the reaction have been zero then?"

"Thirteen to fourteen days ago. Hard to tell, as we have no exact reading," Gernsbeck said.

"And just in case you missed it, that was about the time the glacier collapsed," Justin added—which Elliot had already realized.

"Oxygen," he said, and the men all mumbled in agreement.

"Yes, we came to the same conclusion. The one thing that has now been available in abundance that wasn't before is air. The most likely element from air to produce energy is oxygen. None of us are a nuclear physicist or expert on energy in general, but we've been looking into what method could be used to create such energy," Gernsbeck said.

"Have you used a Geiger counter? Did anyone check if those ruins are radioactive?" Ashra asked from the sideline; Elliot didn't comment. He already knew this was no nuclear reactor, but her question was valid, nevertheless.

"The military did," Gustavsson said.

Elliot turned to his bodyguard. "Private, are you aware of that test?"

Pierce, standing upright and firm, nodded. "Yes, sir. I was present when we tested the area around the ruins for any signs of radioactivity. We could find no unusual readings,"

"Thanks, Private," Ashra said.

"Radioactive material would be used up, so I doubt we're looking at a nuclear reactor," Elliot said.

"Fusion?" Jordan asked.

"Listen." Elliot sighed. "The question is not *what* can create such an electromagnetic field, but what can do so for *twenty-two million years*? We're talking about a way to create energy, a reactor that has not broken, eroded, or been used up in millions of years. A machine like that seems almost impossible. So let's start with the energy source itself. What can provide energy for so long?"

"Wind, oceans," Gernsbeck said right away. "Both not really likely, are they?"

"No," Elliot said. "They're not." He rubbed his temples. "The only way to gain any reliable data on what's in those ruins is by entering them."

"You want to go inside?" Ashra asked.

"Of course, why not?" Elliot said. "There's no radioactivity, and the structure seems to be pretty stable."

"Which is surprising," Gernsbeck said. "It was actually buried under tons of ice for a long time, and as you know, glaciers aren't standing still, they move. Slowly, but in millions of years, it's a significant shift. If anything was purged under them, one would expect it to be squeezed and crushed under the unstoppable force of the glacier. The ruins seem to be rather intact, though."

"Why do you think that is so?" Elliot asked.

"Heat. They must have emanated heat, so the ice around it got thinner," Gernsbeck answered.

"So we have a growing energy source within a ruin that predates humanity by millions of years. Which should have been crushed by the glacier but wasn't." Elliot couldn't help but let a sharp laugh burst from him, it was all so implausible, it left him feeling slightly hysterical. "Gentlemen, does anybody realize what we're talking about here? This is the greatest archeological finding mankind has ever made. It's so unbelievable, we'll need to ship people here to show them, just so they believe us!"

"I doubt Mr. Green will allow that," Jordan said.

"Well, he'll have to. We need to date the structure, map it, analyze every bit of it in every way. We'll need an army of scientists out here," Elliot said.

"I doubt he cares. All he wants is this energy source," Jordan replied. Elliot knew he was right.

"Okay, how long do you need to set up the MRADs?" Elliot asked; Jordan shrugged.

"They're still packed and secured. The software needs to be installed and all that. Ten to eighteen hours at least," Jordan replied.

"Too long. We'll need to go in there ourselves," Elliot replied.

"This could be dangerous. There might be traps," Ashra said.

"After millions of years? I doubt that," Elliot said. "It was a facility of some kind, not a fortress or anything."

"Who will go?" Gustavsson asked; he didn't seem afraid of being chosen.

"Not the weather guy," Jordan joked.

"Or the IT guy," Gustavsson replied.

"We've no idea what awaits us inside there. I need people who have experience in this kind of thing who can keep a cool head when unexpected things happen. Sorry, but I think none of you I know well enough to be sure of that," Elliot said.

"No offense, but what makes you think it's your call?" Gernsbeck shot back.

Elliot understood what he meant. For days, almost two weeks, he had been in charge. He was certainly not qualified, but he had been in charge.

"Because Mr. Green said so," Ashra said, and everyone looked at her. She shrugged. "Sorry, but he calls the shots. We got Elliot here because he knows how to do this. He's a professor of archeology. Experienced in excavating sites and analyzing them. So, he's in charge now."

Gernsbeck's lips grew into thin lines, but finally he nodded.

"I'll accompany you," Pierce said, and all eyes went to the soldier.

"Good. Three people is the minimum for such a . . . trip into the unknown," Elliot said then looked at Ashra. "Ready for more ruins, Ash?"

Ashra forced a smile. "I wouldn't let you go in there alone."

"I know," Elliot said. "So when is nightfall?"

The three men laughed at him. Even Private Pierce's face had a wry expression. Elliot then realized where he was.

"Another few months," Jordan said. "Welcome to Antarctica, Professor. Ice and sun is all we have in here, but we have both in abundance."

****

Boyd's hands clenched to fists, as they rested on his table. He stared at his laptop for a moment, then to Private Pierce who stood next to the door. He shook his head. "There is no other way?" he asked.

Elliot left the talking to Ashra; he knew she spoke his language.

"Boyd, you got us here to evaluate the danger this energy source might pose. How can you evaluate a danger without at least taking a few calculated risks? We'll enter and try to make our way straight to the energy source to get a look at it. Without any visual data it will be almost impossible to evaluate what we're dealing with," she said.

"Understood." He nodded. "But nobody has been in these ruins for . . . maybe no human has ever been in there, right?"

"The ruins were clearly abandoned long before . . ." Elliot paused. "Listen, the dangers on such an exploration are from the environment. Structural damage might make the structure unstable. Falling debris. Slippery ground. Usually there would be a minor danger of infection and toxic gas from rotting materials, but considering how old these ruins are, I doubt we have a problem there."

"I want you to take any precaution you can possibly take. You hear me?" Boyd said.

49

"Of course. We'll return to the surface at the first sign of danger. Leave the job to the drones. But we must try, Mr. Green."

"Okay, you have my permission," Boyd said. "But this is not a vanity mission to make you the first scientist to enter or anything. This is a clear-cut military operation. Your objective is to find and identify the source of the electromagnetic field, identify its nature if possible, and return."

"Of course," Elliot replied, knowing he would document their findings anyway. Boyd didn't realize the scope of this finding, as Elliot did. This was bigger than anything he had ever dreamed of. It was a monumental discovery, and he would let the world know about it, whether the CIA wanted to or not.

"So, the energy source is growing?" Boyd asked.

"That's what Gernsbeck concluded, yes. The field is getting stronger, and logic and science says the amount of energy corresponds to the amount of electromagnetic waves generated, so we have to assume it's growing," Elliot said.

"What do you make of that, Professor? I mean, can this grow indefinitely? If so, how long before it'll become dangerous?" Boyd asked.

"We don't know. When we have a third set of data, we might dig deeper into it. Let's find out what the heck this is," Elliot replied.

"I trust you to keep him out of trouble," Boyd said to Ashra.

"I'll do my best," Ashra replied.

"There is one more thing," Elliot said. "What do you plan on doing with this?"

"The ruins, you mean? I think I made my mission pretty clear," Boyd answered.

"Yes, but sooner or later we must make this known. The scientific community *must* know what we found here. We'll need to get more qualified people on board," Elliot said.

"My mission is threat evaluation, Professor. Once we're sure there's no threat, you can get all your pals up here and start digging around. But first we must make sure this thing is not some sort of problem to us," Boyd said through clenched teeth. "And your scientist honor and ambition won't stand in our way, you hear me?"

"No, sir, of course not," Elliot said. He knew he had just made a promise he might not be able to keep. It was neither his honor nor his ambition driving him right now.

It was his curiosity.

Chapter 5

At least when they went to get dressed, Private Pierce left them alone. Ashra and Elliot had been led to some sort of dressing room that looked as though it had been ripped out of a gym, with lockers and benches lined up.

Ashra got to work immediately, pushing her top over her head and grabbing the violet turtleneck thermal pullover they had been given. Elliot couldn't help it; he stared at her for a second, standing there in her black sports bra. Her body was something he hadn't seen in months, and it still had the perfect shape it always used. As Ashra glanced over to him, pushing her arms into the pullover, he quickly turned his back on her to give her some privacy.

"Nothing you haven't seen before," Ashra said, and he could almost hear the smirk on her face.

"Well, that doesn't mean I should be anything but a gentleman about it," Elliot said, as she pushed her trousers down.

"Not so sure. I think it means you shouldn't be embarrassed about it."

"Well, let's just say then, I'm trying not to be distracted." Elliot laughed and began undressing himself.

"I'm sorry if I'm a distraction." Ashra sounded serious for a moment.

"You've always been my most welcome distraction," Elliot replied; pulling his own shirt over his head.

"You've been working out," Ashra said.

"Yes, a little," Elliot admitted. Actually, he had made it a daily routine to visit the gym. Exercise made his mind clear. For an hour he could concentrate on lifting weights and running, instead of ancient mysteries—and their break-up. Those two topics occupied his mind the rest of the day.

"Are you okay? I mean . . . in Nepal? Have you been all right?" Elliot asked.

"You think this is the moment to discuss it?"

"I don't know. I was just asking . . ."

"I missed you terribly. My job was pretty boring before this. But I'm all right. I . . . guess a lot of people are having a harder time than me," she said. Elliot wanted to reply, but she had something to add. "It was a mistake, Elliot. It was simply a mistake. They lured me back to put me away in an office and let me rot there. When I realized, it was too late. I had lost you."

"Oh, Ashra . . ." Elliot stood up now. "If you had said anything . . ."

"We stopped talking."

"I'm not good with those video things, I know. Guess the tech professor is probably just show."

"No, I got it. I mean, I should have been honest with you. I'm just sorry . . . well, when this all here is over, I would like to talk about London. If you want to . . ."

"Ashra." He stepped closer. "There is nothing I would have loved more than to have this talk . . . but this here is not going to be over. Not anytime soon. This is the Holy Grail of archeology.

54

Whatever we are going to find in there, it'll take *years* to work through this place. Decades probably."

Ashra stared at him, and he felt his inner core melt away like the Antarctic ice, as her brown eyes met his. Then a sad smile appeared on her face, and her hand rested on his chest.

"Well, maybe you'll need a good head of security then? Someone you can trust. Rely on." She shrugged. *Were those tears filling her eyes?*

"Yeah, think Abas is up for the task?" Elliot asked. Ashra burst into laughter.

"You're such an idiot," she said, then looked at her equipment spread on the bench. "We need to get ready."

"I know," Elliot answered; he was desperate to kiss her, but he knew he couldn't. He couldn't distract her from what lay before them. He leaned forward and kissed her forehead gently. "Let's get to our ruin," he whispered.

"One more thing," Ashra said gently.

"Yes?" Elliot asked.

"Don't trust Boyd," she said, looking up at him. "My gut tells me he's not telling us everything. Too few soldiers, too good at answering questions."

Elliot nodded. He totally trusted her. If she said something was off, then it was.

****

They traveled on one of three snowcats to the end of the valley, that led right into the rift. Then they made their descent, driving downwards through endless snow. Elliot felt like they were

55

descending into another world, with those walls hundreds of feet high on both sides. Private Pierce was driving the snowcat, with Ashra sitting in the middle and checking her equipment. Elliot saw how she pulled out a handgun and attached a silencer to the barrel, once she had checked everything else.

"You want to sneak up on some rock formation?" Elliot asked. "Assassinate it?"

"I know how things are with you. It's all perfectly safe until it's not," she said. "You have a silencer for that one?" Ashra nodded at the M5 assault rifle Pierce had pushed between them.

"No, ma'am, not with me," Pierce answered.

"Then leave it here and try to avoid using your handgun in there, if not absolutely necessary. Those things get damned loud, and the echo can hurt you as bad as the bullets," Ashra advised.

"You two have done this before, haven't you?" Pierce asked.

"We have," Elliot answered. "But this will be different, I feel. Those ruins won't be in such a great shape."

They now appeared farther ahead, and he inhaled sharply. From down below, the structures looked way bigger than from above. The giant dish carved into the mountain was so oversized, It looked like one of the satellite dishes from the SETI program, just embedded into the eternal ice, that was now not so eternal anymore. It was clearly made of white stone, which brought up the first question: what was the purpose of this thing? What had they used it for? It seemed like part of some sort of city wall, that shimmered behind the ice. It had to be three-hundred-feet high at least. An enormous structure, engulfing what had been a city behind it. What had these people kept out? Why? What could a civilization like this possibly be afraid of? Had the size been a sign

56

of their power? In an age where nobody built anything, they had built giant reactors to rival whatever Gods they believed in.

"Are those walls?" Ashra asked.

"I think they are," Elliot replied.

"What were they trying to keep out? Giant lizards?"

"A bit oversized for dinosaurs, and even if it wasn't, they died out thirty million years before this place here did. I doubt they even knew they existed at that point," Elliot said.

"So you think they were raging wars?" Pierce asked.

"Hard to say. Maybe among each other, like we do. Anyway, this looks like a fortress in a way, right? Like medieval fortresses around cities to defend them. Just a lot higher." Elliot leaned forward.

"So maybe something bigger than dinosaurs existed back then?" Ashra said. "If we didn't even know civilizations existed, maybe we'll find out soon that giant lizards and spiders were real after all."

"Ashra, those things are physically impossible. They couldn't breathe and would starve to death." Elliot laughed. "I should write a paper on Hollywood myths. Sorry, we won't find any Kaija skeletons today."

"A shame, actually," Pierce said; surprising Elliot with his first sign of humor.

"Yeah," Ashra agreed.

"Good. I have a totally scientific-minded crew with me," Elliot said playfully.

"May I ask you a question? Just off the record?" the soldier asked suddenly.

"Sure," Elliot said. "Please ask me anything you want whenever you want, Private. I'm not your superior."

"You said these weren't aliens, but how sure are you? I mean, we humans created cities by centuries of collaboration, but when I see this? The symmetry, the entire set up looks like this was built . . . in one construction," the soldier said.

"We shouldn't make assumptions. It might just look like that, as we have only seen the external part. But only parts of it. Yet, I'm not seeing any signs this is in any way alien. Just because it isn't *human* doesn't mean that whatever built it came from the stars," Elliot replied. He knew the whole alien thing had become popular due to a certain TV show from the nineties, but humanity still knew little about the deep sea, their own past—or what happened before them. We were ignorant toward humanity's own history and the world around us, while fascinated with unfounded rumors of extraterrestrial life.

Elliot was torn from his thoughts as he saw the entrance appear. The narrow high structure seemed to be made of the same white stone as the rest of the ruins.

"Approaching target point one," Pierce declared.

"It's larger than it looks from afar. Higher," Ashra said.

"As if they wanted to lead giraffes in, right?" Elliot said.

"You think giraffes existed in Antarctica?" Ashra asked.

"No, it was a jungle. Giraffes don't live in the jungle." Elliot took his own backpack as Ashra put her pistol away. He realized she had held onto it the whole time. Her gaze was fixed on Pierce. Elliot knew that sort of look. Did she consider him a danger?

If the US Government was their enemy, a gun with a silencer wouldn't be enough, Elliot supposed. But Ashra had always been the careful one.

The snowcat came to a stop, and Elliot pushed the door open. The entrance was a few hundred feet away. It rose up, and at its sides, he saw large blocks under the ice, as if the entire structure was made of these sixty-feet high blocks. Not unlike the pyramids, he thought. The Ancients had built their city based on cubes, but those stood freely, hollow from the inside. Whoever created this place, they had probably used those blocks to create even more elaborate structures.

"So, you have your flashlights?" Elliot asked. "I hope you checked them."

"Of course," Ashra stood next to him.

"It'll get dark inside pretty quickly. Ice doesn't let enough light through. It's good you brought your guns, but on those things your life relies on. Have the backup available. Have batteries where you can find them in the dark. If you lose these, you'll be dead. Your life will end in that cold dark place in there."

Elliot turned to Pierce, who stood a little behind them and was rearranging his flashlights. Elliot waited until he was done, then started to move toward the black maw in front of them, that led right into a twenty-million-year-old ruin. The oldest archeological find in the history of mankind. Which also made it the most mysterious. He was on the verge of writing history. The first man to step into the ruins of . . . he had to laugh as he realized he had missed his chance to name them so far.

"What?" Ashra asked.

"A name. The place needs one, and whoever built it needs one, too," Elliot said.

"The Antarcticians?" Ashra suggested.

"They're the oldest race we know of to exist. I guess they are our world's ancestors. Let's call them the Ancestors. For now," Elliot said. "Also goes nicely with the Ancients."

"You could be more creative, but works for me. So can we go in now or what?" Ashra looked at him.

"Sure," Elliot said.

"Are you nervous, Elliot Brand?" Ashra asked, as he still hadn't taken another step.

"A little, maybe," Elliot admitted. "I better not mess this one up!"

"You won't," Ashra said. "You were born for this." Elliot turned to her, then finally took the next step, moving toward the entrance. His two companions followed him. He heard the gnawing snow crunch as they stepped on it.

****

The darkness seemed to linger between the high walls of the entrance like a black fog. As Elliot turned on his flashlight, he saw he wasn't far wrong with his metaphor. There was steam hanging in the air, reflecting the beam of light as it wandered through it. He felt a wave of heat as he entered and unzipped his jacket.

"I thought we detected no heat spikes?" Ashra said.

"Yeah, that was days ago. It's heated up," Elliot replied. "We need constant monitoring out here."

"Be careful. The ground might be slippery," Ashra said. "Melting snow means the ice comes forth, and when the surface of it melts, the one that is rough and uneven, whatever is under it can be damn smooth."

Elliot nodded. Maybe he was the expert on ruins, but she was the one who had spent her entire life in the cold. Carefully, he stepped further in and realized they were passing the wall now. It was terribly thick. The adjacent walls seemed massive. He took off his glove, touching them gently.

"Cold. Still," he whispered. "What the hell were they afraid of to build walls like that?" The question was more to himself.

"You ruined my giant lizard theory, so your guess is as good as mine," Ashra replied.

Elliot put the flashlight under his arm, squeezing it between his arm and torso. Then he took out the small red box from his belt.

"Sir, what are you doing?" Pierce asked.

"Taking samples to determine the age with, later on. The material and how it dissolved will tell us pretty much exactly how old this place is," Elliot explained.

"Our mission is to identify and evaluate the energy source, sir."

Elliot ignored him, taking out a small scalpel from the box and a veil made of unbreakable plexiglass.

"Exactly what I'm doing, soldier," Elliot whispered. "Exactly what I'm doing."

"Sir, we—"

Ashra was the one to cut him short with a sharp tone. "Private, Professor Brand leads this mission. How he fulfills the mission is his alone to decide. Understood?"

"Private, we won't be able to get too close to this energy source. It's several miles away, and even under perfect conditions, we'll need hours. This sample will tell us how old this place is though and therefore might give us an idea how old this power source is that should have extinguished millions of years ago," Elliot explained. He appreciated Ashra's military approach. She knew better how to deal with these guys, yet he believed in transparency when it came to why his actions were necessary.

"Understood, sir. My apologies," Pierce said.

Elliot gently scratched at the surface of the wall and collected the stone that loosened. He sealed the sample and put it back into the red box, attaching it to his belt. Putting the flashlight back in his hand, he turned to Ashra and Pierce.

"Let's see how it looks inside." He started walking through the corridor leading from the walls inside.

****

They stepped out of the corridor into bright white light. Elliot raised his head, put on his sunglasses, and saw a giant pillar in the center of the ruins. It rose up all the way to the ceiling. On its top, was a giant white sphere of light, pulsating, with large round structures circling around it.

"Please, take pictures of that," Elliot said; in total awe of the sight before them.

"What's that?" Ashra asked. "It looks like a sun."

"It's the source of the energy," Elliot said, peering below, where lay a sea of cones, all the same size, with smooth surfaces. Nothing resembling streets, nor any structures to suggest it had once been a city were visible. The cones were neither lined up, nor in any special order he could make out, but they covered the entire floor of the giant cave. That was what it was. A cave. Ice had melted away by the white light and created the giant hollow, bubble-like cave they stood in. This was not a city. It was something else. Something technical, based on technology and principles entirely different to those of humanity.

"The glacier didn't only break because of melting ice. The structure had already been weakened," Elliot said. Looking up, he saw there were higher levels still partially embedded in thick ice, with stairs leading up there. Stairs three-feet long and only a few inches high. Not suitable for humans, he realized. The same stairs led upwards from where he stood. A long staircase also led down into the hall. He ignored that for now, and his eyes followed the stairs up. There were bridges and openings in the walls, which all led to some sort of platform; the beginning of a long bridge leading from the wall of the cave all the way toward the central pillar.

"You know what this looks like?" Ashra asked as she stood next to him.

"Like a very large ruin following a very strange idea of how to build a city?" Elliot asked.

"No, it looks like a reactor," Ashra said.

"She's right. But there's no security. No machines except this one," Pierce said.

"The machines would, have dissolved ages ago," Ashra said, and Elliot had to laugh. So she remembered the little lecture he and Teller had given her in the Himalaya after all. She was right of course. They had no idea what this place had once looked like. Every bit of technology that had ever been here, was long turned to rust, dust, and disintegrated completely in a humid environment like this. One thing was obvious though. Whoever had built this place had been a technologically advanced civilization. The giant ball of energy floating up there on the pillar was evidence of that.

Elliot turned and saw both Ashra and Pierce waving around their hand cameras Boyd had provided.

"Brand to Green. Are you there, Boyd?" Elliot barked into the radio they had been given. Only static answered. As expected, the walls of ice were far too thick to get a signal through.

"Sir, I have a signal booster with me," Pierce said, pulling his backpack off. He looked nervous, tense—almost fearful. Elliot understood.

"What the hell is this?" Elliot exclaimed. Twenty-two million years and this place pretty much looked like it had been evacuated last week. Elliot knelt in front of the soldier as he got out a black box.

"Are you all right, soldier?" Elliot asked him.

Pierce looked down at him, his eyes were haunted. "I don't know, man. Is it always like this? I mean, I feel like I landed in some sci-fi flick or something." He inhaled. "Sorry, we're trained to handle the unexpected, but this is a little too strange for my taste. I'll be all right. Just give me a second."

"To answer your question, it's not always like this. Nothing I've ever seen—and I've seen a few weird things—has ever, ever been even close to this. Nothing compares!" He laughed. "And I

64

understand why you are feeling like this. I'm not . . . I hold on to my curiosity. Try that."

"What will we do now?" Ashra asked.

"We'll try to get up there, get closer," Elliot looked at the light again.

Pierce suddenly grabbed the back of his own neck. "Something bit me!"

It took Elliot a moment to realize, and a chill crept down his back —there were no insects in Antarctica.

Elliot ordered the soldier to turn around.

"What is it?" Ashra asked.

Elliot ignored her and instead searched for whatever had 'bit' Pierce. Then on his white jacket, he saw something move. It was the same snow white; almost camouflaged. Elliot leaned forward; he ripped the red box from his pocket and opened it. He tried not to lose sight of the tiny, snow-white object moving down the soldier's back. He grabbed the tweezers and went to his knees.

"What is it, Prof? What *is* it?" Pierce asked, his voice high-pitched with fear.

"Don't move!" Elliot said, and with one swift move, he snapped the tweezers forward and plucked the object away

"Elliot, what are you . . ." Ashra asked.

"The magnifying glass, tiny one. In there." Elliot dropped the red box to the ground.

"Sure." Ashra knelt next to him and took the small, magnifying glass out. She handed it to Elliot, who put it right in front of his eyes and used it to examine the small object he was holding. His breath stopped for a moment; his heart skipped a beat. It had six legs, it was thin and silvery; much like a spider, except two legs were missing. In the middle was a small white body, oval in shape, from the center of the body ran a black line. The surface of the thing opened to reveal a black interior.

"What is that?" Ashra asked.

"Yes, what is that? Has it poisoned me?" Pierce asked fretfully.

Elliot shook his head. "The vial, Ashra. Give me an empty vial." He snapped his fingers, pointing to the red box.

Ashra did as he told her. He carefully put the tweezers with the thing attached inside, and quickly sealed it.

"It's some kind of machine," Elliot said. "And it doesn't look millions of years old."

"Am I . . ." Pierce began.

"I think it took a *sample* of you, but we can't be sure. We're aborting this mission and regrouping at the base. You need to be examined properly. Ashra, you'll take the rear this time," Elliot said.

"We abort? But the energy source . . ." Ashra waved to the giant white ball.

"At the first sign of danger, we're ordered to abort. We just encountered an unknown mechanism, and it bit one of our team members. We're aborting," Elliot said firmly.

Ashra nodded, then took out her gun. Turning around, she gave the "city" of domed objects below a long look. "How many of those are down there?"

"No idea, but next time we come here, we'll do it in hazmat suits," Elliot replied as he patted the soldier's shoulder. "Let's go."

They made their way back through the tunnel to the outside. Elliot radioed for the station to prepare a medical examination of Pierce as soon as they were there—and put him in quarantine.

Chapter 6

"Looks like a spider," Jordan said as he leaned forward, squinting at the magnified image of the small white machine that crawled around in the Perspex vial.

"No." Elliot looked at Boyd, Gustavsson, then finally at Gernsbeck. "It looks like an ant. Ants have six legs. Like this." He folded his arms. "Ants also happened to be around nineteen million years ago."

"So were spiders," Gernsbeck said. "But you're right. It looks like an ant."

Ashra stood in the corner and watched them. She knew she didn't have a lot to contribute. This was Elliot's arena, and even he seemed shocked by the discovery. He was hiding it well, but not well enough.

"We need to get this to a lab. ASAP," Elliot said, and the three men with their glasses all made sounds of agreement.

"Out of the question," Boyd argued.

Elliot swiveled around to face him. "Boyd, I understand the need for secrecy, but we're talking about finding a *machine*, a micro-machine the size of an ant that has been designed nineteen-million years ago. This is like if we found Jesus's time machine or King Arthur's DVD collection! It's a fundamental discovery we need to look into, and for that we need experts, specialists who actually know how to deal with this kind of technology. MIT. Tokyo Institute of Technology. Frauenhofer. For Christ's sake, all of them if we have to!"

"Professor, I have my orders. Nothing goes out of this site until we know what we're dealing with. Consider this not only our base of operations, but also a quarantine zone." Boyd replied.

Ashra stepped forward. She understood perfectly well what Boyd had just said. Under the cover of secrecy, he had just made them prisoners.

"We didn't agree to be your prisoner." She folded her arms and Boyd looked at her.

"You agreed to partake in a secret operation, Ashra. As a spy yourself, you should know what that means. Both of you should have known. Secrecy means we don't share anything with anyone. No calls to home, no samples sent out. No information whatsoever shared," Boyd said.

Ashra shook her head. "Remember when I said I have the feeling they're guarding something, but it's not the ruins? It's something at the base? You remember that, Elliot?" Ashra asked, not taking her eyes off Boyd.

"Yeah, I remember," Elliot replied.

"I was right. They're guarding us. Right Boyd? That's what all those guns are for. They're here for us." Ashra stared at Boyd, who sighed deeply.

"Ashra, that's not what this is about. I trust you two. I didn't even know you, but by the files alone I assumed you would understand the situation. This is a profound finding, I agree. One day we'll make it public, sure. By that time, I'll be done with my job, and nobody will ever know I was here. All the glory will go to you, Professor. To you, Dr. Gernsbeck." Boyd shrugged. "For now, my hands are tied. We must handle this in-house."

70

Ashra was about to open her mouth again when she felt Elliot's hand on her shoulder.

"Mr. Green," Elliot began.

"Boyd, please." The CIA man gave him a tight smile.

"Mr. Green, I don't think you understand the gravity of the situation. We have a professor of archeology here. A meteorologist. A geo-physicist and a . . . hacker?" Elliot said.

"IT specialist," Jordan threw in—but was ignored.

"You," Elliot said, "have an energy source out there in a nineteen-million-year-old ruin, which is a ruin eighteen-and-a-half million years older than the oldest ruin ever found. Eighteen-and-a-half-million years!"

"I'm aware of the scientific significance but let me tell you with no unclear words . . ." Boyd began.

"I'm not yet done," Elliot said. "This energy source is growing. It's charging. It produces a magnetic field. The most powerful ever produced by men. It's not the most powerful field on the planet, of course. That's created by our planet itself. For now." Elliot stared at him. "What if this thing explodes? Hmmm? A few trillion tons of ice melting into water? Or what if it starts doing whatever it's here to do? Can we find out what it is? Maybe. Can we stop it?" Elliot shrugged. "I know nothing of . . . electromagnetism. I don't understand the first thing about reactors or energy transfer or whatever it is we need to know. Nobody here does. Or do any of you?" Elliot turned to the others; everybody shook their head.

"So you say this energy source is dangerous?" Boyd said.

"I say we don't know, and you're playing with powers here nobody here understands. We need experts. If you don't allow us

71

to get outside help, I suggest a compromise. Get experts here, like you got us. And get them here fast," Elliot said. "Because this changes everything!" He pointed to the screen.

"What is it? You know, don't you, Professor?" Boyd asked.

"No, I don't know. But I have an idea," Elliot said. "A hypothesis. I'll share it with you when I have some more insight. For now, you can send guards to our doors and shoot us when we try to run away and let us do our job."

Ashra saw the grimace on Boyd's face that betrayed his anger.

"That won't be necessary," Boyd said. "For a hundred miles there's only ice, Professor. And you won't run anywhere. The ruins are here, and you want us to get to the bottom of it as much as I do. But I'll look for an expert, as you suggested."

"Thanks, Mr. Green." Elliot gave him a weak smile.

"Yes, Boyd, too generous of you," Ashra added sarcastically.

Boyd sighed and walked to the door. "I expect a report in three hours," he said. "Don't do an all-nighter. The sun might not go down, but I promise you'll need sleep anyway."

After Boyd left, Ashra turned to the machine. "So, what is it, Elliot?"

"I did a lecture on the use of nano-machines in archeology. I must say they have amazing use cases. I learned a little about how they work and how we imagine them to work in the future. I think what we're looking at is an assembler," Elliot said. "A self-replicating machine. They're the reason why the energy source is still intact after all those years. Those things consume broken comrades and replicate new models of them. Probably once the whole place was swarming with them, but over time they were reduced. Yet, there are still enough to fulfill their primary objectives, keeping the energy source running. For whatever purpose it still has to fulfill."

"So they need oxygen? Is it that why the machine began running again?" Jordan asked.

"No, it's the water," Gernsbeck said. "The melting water. It will contain micro doses of cadmium, aluminum, platinum. Minimal amounts, but with the mass of water melting and the glacier breaking apart, they had everything they needed to replicate. Professor Brand, I think you might be right." Gernsbeck looked at the monitor where the small white ant was crawling around, testing its environment seemingly for any potential exit.

"Are they dangerous?" Gustavsson had been mostly silent, but finally spoke.

"I don't know, but I didn't have the feeling this was a defense mechanism. It was taking a sample, probably to evaluate if we're intruders," Elliot said.

"That would mean they have advanced intelligence. A guiding principle that's capable of specializing single individuals with tasks," Jordan said. "Like a swarm."

Elliot nodded. "We were in there for only half an hour, but yes, I assume from the whole set-up that we're talking about an advanced species with technological capabilities beyond our own. Also, I'm not sure if we have a human-like intellect at work here. The soldier said something interesting. All of this seems too symmetrical. The place wasn't grown; it was made. We might be looking at a whole different kind of intelligence." Elliot said, and the men fell silent for a moment.

"A swarm intelligence maybe. Like an ant tribe?" Jordan said.

"Too early to say, but yes. Maybe." Elliot looked at Ashra. "Are you alright?"

Ashra was only half listening to the conversation. She began to count in her mind the soldiers and weapons she had seen. Because what none of these guys understood, was how far some people would go to ensure secrecy. A few scientists vanishing in Antarctica would be a small price to pay in order to hide a secret like that.

"What's our next step?" Ashra asked.

"I need you to prepare the MRADs, Jordan. We'll use them to have a closer look at the ruins until we know what we face and can enter again ourselves," Elliot said. Jordan nodded and stood, making his way out of the lab with quick steps.

"Gustavsson, how long until the whiteout?" Elliot asked.

"It's approaching much faster than expected. Two storm fronts will hit us, the first one considerably worse. I would say three to four hours and it'll get unpleasant out there," Gustavsson said. "Another six and going out will be suicide."

"That quick? Bloody hell. Well then, I would suggest we work fast, and whoever has nothing to do rests in the meantime." Elliot turned to Ashra. "That would be you."

Ashra shook her head. "I actually have something to do, Elliot." She turned to leave. "Watch your back!"

****

The truth was, no matter how hard working the men were, Ashra had been trained to spend days without—or with a minimum of—sleep, and still function. Resting would be a waste of time, and she wouldn't waste her time. Boyd was slowly revealing what this really was, but still, something felt off. Considering what they had found, she would have imagined an American army here. Either Boyd believed the relatively small team was easier to control and had a better chance of staying hidden—or he had a different reason to keep them so small.

There were a limited number of sources of information around here. Boyd wouldn't give anything away; he was too well trained. The scientists didn't know anything. Jordan passed her with his winter jacket on, on his way to the equipment shed in the second building, she assumed, getting those remote-controlled drones ready. There was also the medical station, where Pierce, their watchdog, was now quarantined; she almost pitied him. He had certainly not signed up for any of this.

The living room was full of soldiers watching a horror movie set in Antarctica on the old TV. She saw no familiar faces there; she did see one familiar face outside the window though. Captain Miller—if that was his name—stood outside and smoked a cigarette. Ashra went to the exit and grabbed her own winter jacket. She opened the door, and cold wind entered; hissing and filling the room with its icy touch. The weather was already getting rougher by the minute. Making her way out, putting her goggles on so she wouldn't go snow-blind, she approached the soldier.

"Can I have one of those?" she asked.

The man turned around; his thumb hooked under the belt that carried his rifle, which was loosely hanging over his shoulder. "They're club cigarillos. Pretty heavy stuff," he replied. "Ma'am." He added the last word with amusement.

"I'm Ashra, and strong stuff is exactly my thing." She smiled. Miller pulled his glove off and brought a wine-red box from his pocket. Inside were ten cigarillos. She took one. Putting the box away, he handed her a lighter. It was one of those torches that gave a concentrated flame. Putting the cigarillo into her mouth, Ashra ignited it and inhaled deeply. She was used to smoking. Undercover missions in Kathmandu nightclubs actually demanded such things.

"Thanks," she said, sitting down on a nearby box.

"Is it true? What Pierce said about the ruins?" the captain asked.

"Is it not forbidden to ask such things, Captain?" Ashra put the cigarillo between her lips again.

"Well, I guess you're out here to ask me stuff. I thought: let's give her a chance to build some trust." He laughed.

"They're unlike anything I've ever seen. Like straight from one of those two hundred million sci-fi movies they do in Hollywood," Ashra said.

"Damnit. Unknown is not good. Not in my line of profession. One of my guys is in quarantine and you've been in there . . . what? Half an hour?" He shook his head.

"Well at least you're not wasting your time. I mean you protect those ruins, right?" Ashra asked, as a cold wind howled over the plains. She drew her jacket tighter.

"Our job is to make sure nobody comes to harm and everything runs smoothly. Quite simple."

Behind them, she saw the second exit door on the far side open. Boyd came out, pulling his hood up. With him was a second figure, who she assumed might be McKenzie, judging from the silhouette. None of the other soldiers she had seen so far were that small. They went straight for the third building, which looked like a depot.

"What's in there?" Ashra asked.

"Stuff," the captain said.

"Like what?" Ashra eyed the soldier. He was wearing his glasses too, but the eyes weren't the only feature of men that gave away their emotions; that rigid smile of his was to mask tension.

"You have to ask that man from the CIA."

"The guy calling the shots here."

"Exactly." Miller said. Ashra watched Boyd for a moment as he passed two patrolling soldiers, then seemed to type something into a panel—so that was where their secrets were buried.

"You're a strange couple, the two of you," Miller suddenly said.

"Me and the professor?"

"Yeah, hard to believe you two aren't only colleagues. Sorry."

"Oh, we *were* a great couple. Believe me." She laughed. "I had my doubts, but seriously? We did great."

"Who fucked it up?"

"I did."

"Sorry to hear that. For what it's worth, he's still into you." Miller stepped closer and sat next to her.

"You're good at reading people, Captain?" Ashra asked.

"Quite good," he said. "Which is why I know you aren't out here to smoke. You wanted to get a feel for me. Which is strange considering we spent a whole flight together. Something has changed, hmmm?"

"Let's say Boyd Green is a man of surprises," Ashra said.

"Oh, I bet he is."

"You trust him?" Ashra looked at the captain as he threw the remains of his cigarillo into the snow.

"I don't have to trust him. He calls the shots. We follow his orders."

"So, you follow his orders? To the letter?"

"Yes, we do." The captain said. "You concerned about him?"

Ashra shrugged. "My job to be concerned. I envy you guys sometimes. Clear cut game you play. They tell you what to do and you do it. My game, the one Boyd plays too, it's often not so clear. We gather information and we then have to make decisions based on that info. Often those are damned hard and lonely decisions."

"You're one of those guys? Intelligence?" Miller asked. "I don't know much about all that...but I figured out you're no scientist— you're way too cute to be one of them."

The doors opened again. A man with a green jacket made his way through the snow toward the helicopter. He turned to them and raised his arms as a greeting.

"Who is that?" Ashra asked as she returned the gesture.

"Mitchell. The helicopter pilot," Miller answered.

"Yeah, our only way out. I mean, not for all of us, obviously. How many people could the heli carry? Five? Six at most?"

"Yeah, it needs a bit of time to get used to this. The middle of nowhere, all alone, and the only person we can rely on is us. I mean, I've been in remote corners of the earth, but this is a bit more extreme," Miller said. Both of them watched Mitchell as he approached his helicopter and started putting a plastic sheet over it.

"Yeah, and a storm is coming." Ashra's head tilted to the sky.

"My second one now. Bad summer they say," Miller said.

"Thanks again," said Ashra, when she was done with her cigarillo. She started walking to the main building.

"You're good!" Miller called after her; Ashra turned. "How you got this thing about the depot out of me. Smart. Now I need to assign guards to keep your curious eyes out of there."

"I'm sorry I'm causing extra work." Ashra shrugged. "See you."

****

The moment she was inside, she ripped her jacket off. So there *was* something in that depot out there. With the red metal coating, it looked like any of the other buildings. Ashra grabbed a pair of binoculars lying around and moved to the window for a closer look. It seemed to be buried in the ice, so no way to tell how much room it actually contained under the surface. With a sigh, Ashra decided to wait for Boyd to come out, for the chance to see him type in his code. It wasn't likely she'd be able to see it, but it was worth a try.

Her plan was disturbed by steps from the corridor. Running. Someone was running. A young soldier pushed his head into the control room.

"Captain Miller? Green? Seen them?" he asked.

79

"Miller is outside. Smoking," Ashra gently put the binoculars down. "What's wrong?"

"Not now!" He ran toward the exit. Ashra slowly stepped into the corridor and looked in the direction the man had come from. She crept out, transferring her handgun from her back, to her belt. She wondered if Boyd had missed that gun, or if he had decided it would build trust. Anyway, she still had it, and in moments like this, she was happy for it.

She passed the next door, and saw through the window that Elliot and Gernsbeck were still working. They didn't seem to be the source of the soldier's agitation. *Good,* Ashra thought, and took another step down the corridor. The door with the white label COMM was open; a strange smell was coming from it. It smelled burnt. That specific smell of burnt plastic a short circuit created. Ashra edged open the door; the entire console was a bunch of flickering lights, with sporadic sparks dancing over it. An axe protruded from it, the blade buried into the console, with all screens showing only static.

"What happened here?" Miller asked as he appeared right behind her.

Ashra stepped into the room and saw blood on the floor.

"Someone's destroyed the communications. Roberts is missing, and I checked the storage. The backup is missing!" The nameless soldier gasped for air as he explained.

"Vanished?" Ashra bit her lip. "Okay, what other possibilities do we have to reach the outside world?"

"Green has a satellite phone, and the helicopter has communication of course," Miller said.

Ashra didn't hesitate before taking off. Running down the corridor, she didn't care for her jacket. She would survive a few minutes outside, but she wasn't sure if the same could be said about Mitchell.

"Where you going?" Miller shouted, following her. Ashra ripped the outer door open and forced her body out into the freezing wind. The snow was soft and high and slowed her down considerably.

"Mitchell!" she cried as she took the corner of the building, running to the blue helicopter resting on the helipad covered by snow. The rotors were slowly turning, probably to de-ice and check they were properly functioning. He couldn't hear her, standing with his back toward her.

On a pathway between the depot and the main base, she saw Boyd and McKenzie carrying boxes to the main building. Boyd dropped his as he saw Ashra and began to wave his hands toward Mitchell; he had a better chance to be seen.

"Mitchell! Get away from there!" Ashra yelled again; she knew it would take at least another thirty seconds to reach him.

Mitchell finally looked up and saw Boyd. He straightened as Boyd waved toward Ashra. Mitchell slowly turned and saw her.

"Mitchell, get away from the helicopter!" she yelled.

"Get away!" Miller screamed now with her, understanding what she suspected.

"What?" Mitchell yelled back, visibly confused.

"Get away from the—" Ashra never ended the sentence.

81

The shockwave of the explosion blew her off her feet; she felt the cold snow in her face as she hit the ground. The thundering blast was deafening. She turned to see the fireball rise into the air like a mushroom. The helicopter had been ripped to pieces; around her parts of it rained down to the ground. She felt Miller's hand around her arm, dragging her away through the snow. He yelled something, but her ears were filled with a long beeping sound.

"The phone, he might not know about the phone—" Ashra mumbled as she got back to her feet. Boyd covered his face as he stepped closer to the remains of the helicopter. Mitchell lay not far away from it, no longer moving, face down in the snow. A large piece of metal stuck out of his back. Ashra freed herself from Miller's grip and struggled to her feet. Her sense of balance was still wobbly, but she managed to stumble over to Boyd. He turned to her as McKenzie and two other soldiers came running with fire extinguishers in their hands. Ashra reached Boyd and grabbed his jacket, to stop herself from falling over.

"Your phone! Where is it? The satellite phone?" she gasped.

"What?" Boyd looked at the helicopter.

"The radio is gone and so is the backup. So where is that damn thing?" Ashra asked.

Miller suddenly arrived and helped support Ashra by holding her shoulders.

"What?" Boyd looked at Miller, then began stomping through the snow to the main base. Ashra shrugged Miller off, as she felt her ability to stand independently return. "Secure the scientists and all vital systems," Ashra said.

She saw Miller's face and knew what he was thinking: *Was she now giving the orders? This mid-twenties Nepalese girl? Damned if she was.*

"Go, dammit! Before anything else is lost!"

Miller turned and began running after Boyd. Ashra stood there for a moment, catching her breath. She saw McKenzie staring at her, her hands holding a large box. Ashra wondered why she was staring. Did she suspect Ashra? Ashra had been the only one trying to save Mitchell. The dead man still lay in the snow only a few meters away.

"Are you alright?" McKenzie finally asked.

"Yes, soldier. I'm okay." Ashra nodded and grit her teeth together. She could hear a bit now, but her ears hurt. So did her back, which had taken most of the impact.

"I need you to come with me now," McKenzie said, gently putting the box down.

Ashra saw her hand go to her gun. "Of course. But someone killed a member of our mission, and that someone could have been you. So if you're not ready to use it, I suggest you take your hand off your gun or I swear, I'll shoot first and ask questions later. Understood?" Ashra raised a brow.

McKenzie just stared at her. "Ma'am, I have no idea what you Nepalese guys can do, but I assure you, intimidating me won't work. You need to come with me now!"

"Wait, give me a second chance, okay?" Ashra said.

"Second chance at what?" McKenzie asked. With one fluid move, Ashra brought out her own handgun and pointed it right at her head. The other woman didn't even have time to draw.

"At intimidating you. Better now?" Ashra asked, stepping forward and holding the pistol with the silencer still attached into the woman's face. She slowly grabbed her handgun, and with one hand, ejected the magazine and pushed it into her belt.

"This is—"

"This is what one calls securing a suspect. Let's go. I guess they want us all to go to the mess?" Ashra said. McKenzie nodded, with no choice but to go ahead.

Chapter 7

Elliot and Gernsbeck entered the mess as the others gathered. Boyd stood at one side, with Miller next to him; they both looked up as they entered.

"Where's Ashra?" Boyd asked right away. Elliot could only shrug. His eyes rested on the soldiers, who one by one stepped forth and laid down their weapons. First their rifles, then their handguns; finally, their knives.

"What's going on?" Elliot asked. "I heard an explosion." Gernsbeck withdrew to the door, but before he got there, he was pushed aside.

"We got a saboteur and a murderer in our base," Ashra said and pushed McKenzie to the other soldiers, her gun pointed at her head.

"Ashra, you have to hand over your—" Boyd began.

"I was with him." Ashra pointed at Captain Miller.

"I can confirm that, sir. We smoked outside. We saw you leaving the main building," Miller said, and Boyd nodded.

"Professor? Please lock the door. McKenzie? Grab an assault rifle and join us," Boyd said, then waved to Ashra. Her face was etched with unease.

"What did they sabotage?" Asking her as she passed, Elliot knew she shouldn't answer.

Leaning forward, she whispered to him. "Helicopter and radio. Killed Mitchell." The meaningful look she gave Elliot indicated they had a problem. Nodding at her, he went to the door and did what he had been told. He turned the key and took it out of the keyhole. Ashra grabbed an assault rifle, as did the female soldier who had brought him here; McKenzie.

"So, ladies and gentlemen, it seems we have a problem," Boyd said. "Someone used an axe to destroy our radio, stole the backup system, then seemingly blew up the helicopter, killing Mitchell. Also, my satellite phone has been stolen. In our midst is a traitor, murderer, and saboteur." Boyd clenched his teeth. "I had a beer with Mitchell at Concordia base. He had a wife and kids. So I take this rather personally. I make the traitor an offer. It's a one-time offer. If he steps forward now, I'll let him stay alive, get into custody, get a fair trial and all that." He spread his hands and Ashra watched the crowd. Jordan and Gustavsson huddled near Elliot and Gernsbeck, and he could see they were scared.

"Okay, I make no promises if we find you ourselves, bastard. We'll go now one by one, identifying who has an alibi and who doesn't." Boyd tilted his head slightly, as if he was fighting a stiff neck.

"Professor?" he asked. "Where were you and with whom?" Elliot saw all eyes turn to him.

"I was with Dr. Gernsbeck in the laboratories for the last two hours. Since coming back from the ruins," Elliot said.

"Can you confirm that?" Boyd looked at Gernsbeck.

"Yes, sure. Of course." Gernsbeck nodded. "We were together the whole time. Didn't even have a toilet break. Mentioning it, I could—" He shrugged and everybody seemed amused.

"You'll need to restrain yourself a little longer," Boyd answered. "You two can join us on this side of the room; grab a gun if you want to," Boyd said. Both Elliot and Gernsbeck didn't take him up on this privilege. Gernsbeck stepped behind the line of armed soldiers, and Elliot moved next to Ashra. She handed him a handgun; probably the one from McKenzie.

"It's empty. Just to make you look armed," she whispered. Elliot took it and nodded.

Boyd continued the questioning. Most soldiers had been in teams. The patrols had been two men, most had been here in the mess and could vouch for each other. When Boyd was done, only four people remained on the side of the suspects. Jordan had been alone in the equipment room, working on the drones. Gustavsson had been in his room, trying to sleep. Pierce had been in the medical station, alone as the medic restocked it, and one soldier had been on the toilet. They all could be lying and would have had time and access to the damaged radios and Boyd's office which had been broken into. The helicopter, Elliot thought, was a different topic. Actually, a bomb had been used from what he heard. A bomb that could have been planted there at any time. Elliot looked around and saw the soldiers, all now with uneasiness on their faces.

"Private Jackson, Private Pierce, you two will be isolated to your quarters, together. Miller? I want a guard there twenty-four seven," Boyd said. Miller nodded, and both men saluted. "Gustavsson and Jordan, you two . . ."

"We need them," Elliot said. "At least Jordan needs to prepare the drones of the MRAD system."

"You aren't able to do so?" Boyd asked.

87

"No, I mean, yes, but I would need much longer. I've never worked with an operational system. The whiteout is coming, and we don't know how much time we have before the situation . . ." Elliot had no idea how much the soldiers knew, but he had to make his point, ". . . becomes critical. I suggest he continues his work under supervision."

"Agreed," Boyd said. "We don't have men in abundance, and we already run double shifts. Can you help out, Ashra?" He looked at the young woman. Ashra nodded.

Elliot could hardly imagine the two men sneaking around and planting bombs, but what did he know? The truth was, they were now in danger. Someone was here to keep them from exploring the ruins, and he had no idea who or why. But whoever it was, that person went over dead bodies to fulfill their mission.

"Everybody else, from now on will only move in pairs. Toilet, work, patrols, checkups, medical station, all of it. Always in pairs. Always two in the same damn room," Boyd said. "Do you understand?"

"Yes, sir," the soldiers said with one voice.

"Professor, Ashra, Miller, you'll stay here, and the rest of you move out. Miller, you keep an eye on our suspects." Boyd said. Elliot folded his hands and watched all the soldiers leave. When they were gone, only the soldier, the CIA man, Ashra, and himself remained. Nobody said a word for a moment.

"What am I doing here? I mean, you guys are experts in this, but I'm a professor of archeology," he said.

"You're also probably the smartest person in this station," Boyd said. "I thought you might be useful at solving the riddle."

Elliot inwardly groaned. People always expected an academic to be some sort of Sherlock Holmes, and even if he always said archeology was like detective work, he really didn't think he would be all that helpful.

"Thoughts?" Boyd said.

"We have four suspects. Let's keep a tight control over the four, let them do their job under constant surveillance, then we fly them out. Our experts can interrogate them," Miller said.

"And how do you want to call the extraction team?" Ashra asked. "We are cut off, or do you have another communication line hidden somewhere?"

Boyd shook his head. "No, we had four systems. More than enough."

"But at some point, someone will come, right?" Elliot said. "If we stay silent."

"Seven days," Boyd answered, stroking his clean shaved chin. "If we stay silent for seven days, the beta team will be deployed, and it needs another day to get here.".

"Seven days!" Ashra laughed. "If we don't find who did that, we might not last that long."

"What are we talking about? I mean, who has an interest in sabotaging us and this mission?" Elliot asked.

"A foreign power? A private interest group?" Ashra said.

"Everyone here was handpicked. Checked several times. Everyone except you two, passed the highest level of clearance. No relations to other governments or anything indicating they might be involved with any shady organizations," Miller said.

"Well, it's the nature of deep agents to pass such tests. It's their whole point." Boyd said. "We've narrowed it down to four men."

"I doubt my men are under any real suspicion," Miller said.

"Why?" Elliot asked.

"Because they're all soldiers of the US special forces, ran through millions of background checks, and have served their country on multiple occasions."

"Doesn't mean they couldn't be corrupted," Ashra said. "An alcohol problem? A new lover? Money? Debts?" Ashra offered some examples. "The helicopter was blown up using an explosive device. I guess we'll find explosives missing when we check them. Your men probably have been trained with explosives?"

"Yes, both," Miller admitted.

"They also know how to move silently, plant a bomb, and they knew the routines of the patrols and all that," Boyd added.

"So looks like we have two main suspects," Ashra said. "Pierce and this . . . Jackson?"

"Pierce is an expert with explosives. He's had advanced training," Miller added.

"Oh, I don't think we have two main suspects, or even four." Elliot raised his voice, and everyone turned to him. The longer he thought about it, the less sure he was that what they had done would solve their problem.

"Elaborate?" Boyd asked.

"We assume it's one traitor. Why not two? Would explain how they covered all the ground so fast. Then they gave each other an alibi," Elliot said. "It would make sense. A lone traitor would have known we would isolate all suspects."

Everyone looked at him for a moment, then Boyd hissed air through his teeth. "Damnit," he said.

"They couldn't get to two of my . . ." Miller began.

"Of course, they could," Ashra said. "That's what experts do."

"No, the whole operation was organized on short notice. Miller is right," Boyd said. "One of them must have been a sleeper. Smuggled into the team somehow on short notice."

"And we're willing to bet our lives on it?" Ashra asked, folding her arms and eyeing Boyd.

"How long do you need? How long do you need to finish your studies, Professor?" Boyd asked.

"Thirty years," Elliot said.

"I'm serious . . ." Boyd replied.

"I'll try to get the answers as fast as possible, but without additional help, it's not clear if we can do it at all," Elliot said. "But is that truly the question?"

"What do you mean?" Boyd asked.

"Well, *why* has the traitor cut us off? I think that's truly the question we need to ask ourselves." Elliot put to them. "Did he want to slow us down, or does he have a plan? Something to stop us for good?"

"What about the snowcats? We could fill them with petrol and drive to the next research outpost?" Ashra suggested.

"Good idea, except it's Russian," Miller said.

"Oh man, great." Ashra shrugged.

"Okay, we go to red alert. I want everything that burns and explodes secured and guarded by five men at all times," Boyd said.

"That will mean I can barely keep up all our other assigned tasks," Miller said.

"I'm aware of that. Cut it down to the bare minimum," Boyd said. "When the whiteout comes and that bastard sets the base on fire, we'll freeze to death out there."

Elliot sighed, put his hands into the pockets of his snowsuit, and made his way to the door.

"What are you doing?" Boyd asked.

"Going to work," Elliot replied and turned halfway. "I think we have a little more time than before." Without waiting for an answer, he made his way to the door. Outside, Jordan, Gustavsson, and Gernsbeck awaited him. They all looked very excited and had strange smiles on their faces.

"What is it?" Elliot asked, and he heard Ashra's steps right behind him.

"You *have* to see this," Gernsbeck said, and turned to walk to the lab. Elliot looked at Jordan and Gustavsson who both nodded in agreement. Elliot followed Gernsbeck who was already standing at the computer.

"What the hell is that?" Ashra asked, staring at the screen.

"Look at the tweezers," Gernsbeck whispered. They looked as if they had corroded. Their tips were . . . vanishing. The white ant crawled up and down them and seemed to always go to the tip then crawl back to a small white ball on the ground of the vial.

"It's trying to replicate!" Elliot gasped. "I was right."

"Makes sense. It has a mission, and when it can't fulfil it, it returns to its basic function. Which is replication," Jordan said and folded his arms. "Makes sense for a rudimentary drone intelligence. Whatever its energy source is, it'll be limited. Limited life cycle. The least it can do is replace and create a fresh drone so the swarm doesn't run out of them."

"So over the years, more and more specialized drones died without replicating. Creating a problem, as less and less of those small guys were around to do the work," Elliot said.

"Just as you said," Gernsbeck said.

"When will the MRAD be ready?" Elliot asked Jordan, without turning his eyes away from the little ant. On the screen, it made its way from the tips of the tweezers down to the little white bowl.

"An hour," Jordan said.

"When is the whiteout coming?" Elliot turned now to Gustavsson.

"It's still speeding up, but for four hours or so we should be good. And...Professor?"

"It's Elliot," Elliot said.

"You think one of us is the . . . you think one of us might have done this to Mitchell?" Gustavsson asked.

It was Ashra who answered for him. "Whoever did this was skilled with explosives. So a soldier is more likely, but yes, Gustavsson. We're all suspects until we know who it was."

"I thought you guys have been cleared?" Jordan asked.

"No, not really. Now go to work." Elliot straightened himself. Jordan and Ashra exchanged a look, then vanished through the door.

"You went to the toilet," Elliot said to Gernsbeck, keeping his arms folded.

"Barely enough time to break into two rooms, steal stuff, hide it and plant a bomb, I guess. I just had a piss," Gernsbeck said. "You were alone, too."

"Yes, I was. But I know I didn't do this."

"Neither did I, Professor," Gernsbeck said then looked at Gustavsson.

The overweight little man pushed his glasses up his nose. "I didn't do nothing!" he said, raising his hands.

"What about Boyd?" Gernsbeck said. "He wanted us to not contact the outside world and now suddenly we're not able to anymore? Seriously, that's not a coincidence."

"Seems he was outside with McKenzie," Elliot said.

"Well, he could have had an opening, right? The bomb he could have planted days ago, the phone was in his possession all the time, and when did they last check the backup system was even there? All he needed was probably twenty seconds to grab the axe and ram it into the console of comm." Gernsbeck shrugged.

"How do you know that's what was done?" asked Gustavsson.

"I passed the room on my way to the mess. Door open. I saw it; it's still stuck there," Gernsbeck said.

"Let's go to work." Elliot interrupted their conversation. "Let's leave this to the professionals, okay?" He turned his eyes to Gernsbeck and Gustavsson. They were both suspects, of course. He just had a hard time imagining either of them being a trained sleeper agent for a foreign power. Then again, the whole point of sleeper agents was probably to look nothing like them.

Chapter 8

They had all assembled in the lab. Boyd was there, standing right behind the line of laptops now resting on the desk. Jordan and Elliot sat in front of it, and Ashra had spent the last hour watching Elliot work. It was as if nobody was out there to kill them all. For him, there were only the ruins now and those white drones he had sent toward them. The footage of them was visible on the five laptops that served as a makeshift control station.

Gernsbeck sat to the side, with Gustavsson next to him, sipping on a can of Coke. Miller was there. McKenzie. Both wearing sidearms and trying to look as if they weren't here to shoot any traitor who might spontaneously reveal himself.

"So walk us through the process, Professor," Boyd said and unfolded his arms.

Elliot turned in his chair and she saw that professor look on his face. The satisfaction as he saw his audience, then his outstretched hands to get their attention.

"It's quite simple. You all know drones, and you know how they work? You all know they can carry a camera. So, these five drones, each carrying one camera. They create a mesh network; do you know what this is?" He looked around. Ashra was sure some of the group did, but nobody spoke up. "The internet is a connection of millions of computers. The mesh network is the same, but it has only a few participants, like our five drones who can exchange data through it. This exchange allows us to create a detailed map of the place, as any drone recognizes obstacles and walls and transmits those ovations to all other drones, leading to a map that is slowly building as they fly through the area. The same time we receive footage, that will allow us to later create a full 3D map of the place. We'll send the drones to the entrance. Right now, they're on autopilot, reaching their destination in three minutes. We'll enter without any further ado, as we only have ninety minutes of battery on each, and we need twenty minutes for the way there and back. That means we have fifty minutes of four drones to map the city. The fifth drone we will control directly and fly up straight to the energy source to have a closer look at the structure up there, and probably find what we are looking at here," Elliot explained. "Any questions?"

"Proceed, Professor," Boyd said, before he threw Ashra a glance; as if monitoring she was still there. Her placement near the door hadn't gone unnoticed.

"We're arriving at the entry," Jordan said and pushed his glasses up. He typed into the laptop in front of him.

"Good. Initiate the mapping protocol, give us number one on the big screen, and let all others run on auto," Elliot said.

"Will fifty minutes be enough to make the entire place? It was huge," Ashra said from the door. On the only large computer screen, they saw the drone dive into the darkness of the entrance.

"Not even close. We get what we can and have to work with that until the drones are recharged. We'll do this all week," Elliot said.

"All week." Boyd sighed and repeated the words.

"Yes, all week, Green," Elliot answered. The drone broke free of the darkness and entered the main cave. Ashra had seen it with her own eyes, but even she felt an undeniable feeling of awe as the giant cave became visible, the enormous pillar in its center towering over everything, with the brilliant white, pulsating ball encircled by metal beams on the top.

"What the . . ." the words escaped Gernsbeck's mouth.

"Welcome to Antarctica," Elliot proclaimed, and the drones on the other screens began to spread to all sides.

"Bring it up to two-hundred-feet and approach," Elliot ordered Jordan, who began typing, and the drone started to rise in response.

"See those temperatures?" Gernsbeck pointed at a screen.

"Yes, almost ten degrees," Elliot said. "We had no more than eight."

"It's heating up. The walls are reflecting the heat," Gernsbeck said.

"With an energy source like this, the whole room should be boiling," Gustavsson added. He had pulled his chair closer. "No encasement. No hull. The core lies bare."

"What does that mean?" Boyd asked.

"I'm not an expert, but usually energy is harvested by a shell surrounding the core. Water is made into steam, and turbines or dynamos are powered. This looks like the energy is just there. I wonder what keeps it in its form?"

"An electromagnetic field," Elliot replied.

Gustavsson looked at him and laughed. "You're right! That must be it!"

Ashra had to smirk. *As always, the smartest guy in the room.* The drone now rose up the pillar.

"What's this made of? Looks like marble or basalt or something like that," Boyd said, now also leaning forward to the screen. They looked like a gang of kids putting their heads together to coordinate a prank.

"I bet this one was coated with some sort of hull once," Elliot said. "See those marks? I guess that's where the metals were locked into the structure. Those holes, like vents."

"We've reached the top. Shall I go closer?" Jordan asked.

"No, we have no idea how strong the magnetic field is. We don't want to lose the . . . wait." Elliot snapped and pointed to the screen. "Move twenty degrees left."

Jordan typed, and the drone responded. Ashra now stepped closer too. She saw a bridge at the side of the giant pillar. It was hanging free without any railing. It led to a long, high door in the side of the pillar.

"What is that?" Boyd asked.

"A way into the machine," Elliot said. "We can fit through this, can't we?"

"Barely, I'd say," Jordan said. "Three-feet wide, needs a little piloting skill to get in there."

"I have full trust in your abilities," Elliot said, and the drone accelerated to make its way to the shaft at the side. Inside, Ashra saw a blue light.

"It's powered," she said.

"Yes," Elliot said. "It seems to have some sort of lighting system."

The drone approached the slit in the wall that had a frame like the main gates they had used to enter. A miniature version of the main gate. She saw blinking reflections of light behind the entrance, then suddenly the screen went dark.

"What happened?" Boyd asked.

"What I was afraid would happen. We went into the field. The electromagnetic field fried our drone!" Elliot leaned back and ran a hand through his hair.

"Can we send another?"

"Would be the same result. The machines aren't shielded against that kind of energy," Elliot explained.

"So how do we get in there?" Boyd asked.

"The old-fashioned way," Ashra answered. "You want to go into the ruins again, don't you?"

"They're warm enough to wear hazmat suits in there now to protect us from our little friends. Yes, I think we must get back inside again." Elliot nodded.

"We'll discuss this later. Conclude the mapping, then we should analyze the footage," Boyd said.

"We have time. Looks like the storm is coming soon," Ashra said, as another howling wind rattled the building.

"It isn't a bad one, historically speaking," Gustavsson said.

"But are they often in summer?" Elliot asked him.

"Not unheard of. But pretty rare," Gustavsson said.

"What are you thinking, Elliot?" Ashra asked.

"I was just wondering . . . this storm is becoming faster and faster as it approaches. Clouds are charged with electrical energy, especially those who are part of a storm. I was wondering if our friend is drawing the storm to us." Elliot looked at Gustavsson, who shrugged and took his glasses off to polish.

"That . . . that is actually entirely possible," he said. "I mean theoretically. There's never been a field this strong, but the theory of weather manipulation is based on creating magnetic fields to guide clouds into the desired position. Professor, you might be right."

"Fascinating, but I think we need to find out how this thing can be turned off. We should focus on that task. Conclude the mapping and get back to me."

"Will do," Elliot said, and Boyd turned and left the room.

Ashra watched him leave, then noticed the two soldiers had remained here. Elliot seemed not to bother.

"This is the way up. See? Here we can go around, then up there to the highest level. Let them scan the area, if we find any passage through this area, we'll be able to reach the pillar," Elliot instructed Jordan.

"Twenty minutes will be tough," Jordan said.

"Try." Elliot stood up. He smiled and circled the long lab table on which the laptops rested. Ashra followed him.

"What's on your mind?" she asked.

"I'm not sure who to trust." Elliot sighed and looked at her. "Neither do you."

"I trust you." Ashra winked at him.

"And I trust you, but the two of us . . . that's not a lot in a place filled with those," Elliot whispered.

"You're afraid someone will steal this, aren't you?" Ashra could see it, now that he let his mask slip for a moment.

"This is the most dangerous discovery imaginable that we've found here. An energy source like this? Those little machines? In the wrong hands, those could do . . . *incredible* damage," Elliot said.

"Every technology humanity has ever found was weaponized, Elliot. You know history better than me; you know that all too well." Ashra put her hand on his arm.

"Yeah, now a question. Was that the same nineteen-million years ago?"

Ashra heard steps from behind. Both turned, and Jordan stood there fumbling with his hands.

"Am I disturbing anything?" he asked.

"We're discussing the potential next trip to the ruins," Ashra said, as the better liar of the two.

"Okay, the drones are on their way back here. The mapping is complete," Jordan tilted his head. "I think I found a passage to that room."

"Thanks, Jordan." Elliot nodded. "Can you get the footage on my laptop? I think I would like to see it before I get some rest."

"Sure." Jordan walked away again, leaving Ashra and Elliot alone.

"Boyd is hiding something in the depot. I'll try to find out what," Ashra said. "He was there when the helicopter blew up."

103

"What do you think?" Elliot asked.

"No idea, but I'm going to find out."

"I'm so glad you are here," he finally said. "Having my back."

"Always, Professor Brand, always." Ashra smiled, and she had the overwhelming urge to kiss him, but knew nothing would be less appropriate at that moment. She quickly stepped away so as not to be tempted, and walked back to the team.

They were all working; nobody realized as she passed them and left the room, violating the rule of two Boyd had created. He himself had left alone. The corridor was empty. With the equipment guards doing double shifts, almost no soldiers were left off duty. Everybody was patrolling, sleeping, or guarding the equipment.

Ashra turned to the mess and entered. It was dark. They had closed the blinds. She wondered why? Probably to finally get some darkness or watch a creepy horror movie. She appreciated the absence of the unending sunlight and walked over to the fridge. Opening it, she took out a sandwich and a bottle of water, she bit into the sandwich and opened the plastic bottle.

"Ma'am?" The voice made her head snap up. Her hand moved to the pistol in her belt. Pierce stood there in the dim light and raised his hands.

"I thought you guys only move in pairs now?" Ashra asked. He kept his distance. She couldn't see him wearing a weapon.

"My tandem partner is sleeping, and I thought I'd take the opportunity to talk to you." Pierce came one step closer, and Ashra felt her fingers close around the grip of her gun.

"Are you trying to scare me, Private?" Ashra asked.

"I doubt I could. No, I'm the one who's scared. Because I planted the bomb at the helicopter. C-4. Remote controlled."

Ashra drew her gun, armed it, and pointed it right at the head of Pierce.

"I acted on Miller's orders!" Pierce quickly said.

"*What?*" she blinked in irritation.

"And he acted on Boyd's orders."

Ashra stared at him for a moment, then lowered her gun. "Damn."

Pierce nodded. "I know. I'm afraid he's going to blame it on me now. But it was him who . . ."

Ashra stared at Pierce. At least someone was starting to speak the truth.

"Do you know what's in the depot?" she asked.

"No, I don't have that kind of security clearance," he answered.

"You should probably go to sleep now before your tandem partner wakes up." Ashra sighed. She knew what she had to do, and she couldn't even risk warning Elliot about it.

****

Ashra checked that Miller and McKenzie were still with the scientists. Then she slipped down the corridor and knocked at the door of Boyd Green's self-declared office.

"Yes?" he answered. Ashra opened the door, drawing her pistol once again, keeping it behind her back as she smiled upon entering.

105

"Wondered if we could have a word?" Ashra asked.

"Sure." Boyd nodded.

He rested with his head on his hands sitting behind his long empty lab table. He looked up and tried to give her a confident smile.

Ashra wandered in and sat opposite him. His eyes went to her arm held behind her back.

"What do you have there, Ashra?" Boyd asked.

Ashra revealed the gun, setting it on the table, her hand still around the grip, her finger on the trigger.

"What is this going to be? You want to kill me? How will you get away with that?" Boyd asked, and his hands moved for a second to the side; probably to his jacket where she assumed his weapon was. He would never be fast enough to get it, and they both knew it.

"I could scream," he said.

"You could try," Ashra replied with a clinically icy voice.

"I see you're serious about this," Boyd said.

"I know about the charge. The C4 you had Pierce attach to the helicopter," Ashra said.

"So much for those stone-cold professionals and their secrecy, hm? Stupid kid," Boyd answered. "I understand what this looks like, but I assure you it had nothing to do with . . . I didn't activate it."

"Then why did you put it there?" Ashra asked.

"A safety measurement. We've found the world's biggest energy source here, Ashra. Do you have any idea what this means? Could solve the energy crisis. A billion, trillion dollars find. I was concerned someone would try to get away with it. Someone would betray us. So I had safety measures in place. Every snowcat has a tracker on it. The helicopter had a charge. The remote control rested in that drawer over there. Together with the satellite phone. Locked." He pointed to a drawer with shattered wood clearly visible on the front panel. "He took them. Both of them. Then he used them to blow the helicopter up."

"The traitor," Ashra said.

"Yes. He must have seen Pierce. Hard to sneak around outside in broad daylight, I guess. Damn sun. Could go down for a few hours at least, hmmm?" He folded his arms and tilted his head. "I didn't think of an internal enemy. I would have secured it better if that idea had even crossed my mind."

"You should have told us," Ashra said.

"Oh, c'mon. We both know it's not our nature to admit to things. People in our line of business have secrets. I decided to keep this one," Boyd said.

"Well, yours killed Mitchell." Ashra put her gun away.

"Someone used it to kill him, yes. I'll find whoever did that and kill him. No, I guess now that we two know neither of us is the traitor, I think I'll let you find him."

Ashra thought about Pierce. He snuck around alone in the base and had just deflected any suspicion from himself to the others. The truth was, he had known that the bomb was there.

"We need to keep an eye on Pierce," she said and stood up.

107

"He won't be allowed to carry arms for now," Boyd said. "But he seems to have a talent to slip away. Maybe we should do something about that." Ashra left the room, actually believing him. Of course, he had told only half the truth. The bomb was also there in case any of them had tried to flee.

As she left the room, she wondered how far Boyd would go to keep his secret. If he didn't want any of this to become public, a member of a foreign security agency and a bunch of scientists would become a problem once he didn't need them anymore. Nobody knew they were here. She would need to be very careful from now on or this icy desert would be her grave. Ashra had always imagined she would die in the ice one day—but hadn't planned to do so this early. Certainly, she wouldn't let Elliot die here. If Boyd planned to get rid of his witnesses, she needed to be prepared to get rid of him, without the soldiers executing them afterwards.

Chapter 9

The storm hit them with full force a few hours later. The howling became a constant sound as the wind raged against the metal structure of the building. These things were created to withstand the worst of the worst storms, but Elliot felt like any second they could be blown away. After a day without sleep, he now found the wind to be terrifyingly effective in keeping him awake.

He had locked the door and additionally barricaded it with a chair under the doorknob. Ashra had advised him to do so. He knew when it came to counter-espionage, she was probably the expert.

His mind wasn't able to concentrate on the traitor in their midst, though. Even in the face of being potentially murdered, all he could think of were the ruins.

Nineteen-million years; long before the earliest predecessor of man had split from the apes. That had happened later in the epoch known as the Miocene era. The early stages, the Agenian age, had been defined by spreading mammals that became the predominant life form on the planet. The first bears, beavers, and horses arrived in the ecosystem. Giant whales roamed the seas, undisputed by any other creature. In that age, something had developed, and it had developed to a degree that it had been able to create a reactor and miniaturized machines. It was a sensation unlike any other. A matter of pure luck this one city—and God only knew how many there had been—hadn't been subject to wind and water but encapsulated in a giant glacier to be preserved longer than any other structure on the planet. It would have stayed down there for millennia to come, hadn't humankind heated up the planet so badly the eternal ice itself began to melt.

The Ancients in the Himalaya had been a sensation, but this here was much more than that. This was a total gamechanger in the history of this planet. It wasn't archeology; it was something way more profound. Nobody here believed him, but Elliot knew enough about this age to know it wasn't very likely that the inhabitants of this place had developed from apes. It took another few million years for apes to actually appear and spread over all continents. No. It was very likely an entire civilization had existed that had access to technology and built this giant city that had actually developed from another species. The ancestor of all intelligent life on the planet might have not been human; an idea that was strange and dangerous at the same time. How would humanity react when they found out they weren't the first? Humanity didn't take being degraded to number two very well, actually. That was his experience.

Then again, would anybody care? Would they not be too busy fighting over control of this technology? That was what really kept him awake. Maybe Boyd was indeed right. Maybe getting a thousand scientists down here meant there would be a thousand reports, and how long would it take until one of the states thought it was too dangerous to share this with the others? Would the others tolerate it? Could they even? No radioactivity, and according to the magnetic field, the largest most powerful energy source on the planet, seemingly not burning any fuel. For a technology like this, wars were fought. Actually, they had been fought for far less.

In his search for answers, he had always pushed forward. Never had he considered the consequences of his findings. Yes, the Ancients in Nepal had artifacts that hinted they might have had a hand in the creation of humanity. What would it do with humanity if they found out? The belief the world was better off with the truth had always been his shield all these years. The truth was, he had never questioned if that was actually right. He

110

had never considered the truth might be harmful. Religions might be put into question. People might despair upon realizing how insignificant they had really been, An accidental by-product of a slave breeding program. Here it was different though. The knowledge hidden in these ruins was way more dangerous. It was actually knowledge that could be used for practical purposes. Unlimited energy sounded like a blessing to mankind, but what if history repeated itself? What if by learning of their methods and technology, humanity would enter the same path and face the same end? Had the Ancients known about the Ancestors? Had they fallen into the same trap? Was it a long line of repeating cycles that ended each time with the extinction of the species that was predominant on this planet? Elliot felt he couldn't treat such questions lightly. Truth wasn't enough. He had to mind the consequences. He had to take responsibility. Especially because there was nobody else here who could. The thought slowly led him into a deep sleep.

****

Elliot was shaken from his dreams by a loud sound. Metal on metal, clonking as two objects hit each other. He opened his eyes and slowly sat up. Ashra's room was right next to his, but he heard nothing from there. He wasn't even sure if she was in her room after all. The wind growled again. Elliot opened the blinds and looked out of the window. He understood right away why it was called a whiteout. There was indeed only white. He could not see beyond a foot from his window.

He had a choice; stay in here and let someone else figure out what had made that sound, or go and find out himself—as if he had ever let anybody else satisfy his curiosity. With a deep sigh that was almost a complaint against himself, he pushed away the chair and unlocked the door. He opened it a little and peered out. The corridor was dark, as most blinds had been shut—a security measure in case of a snowstorm, he had been told. They should do that every night, because it felt almost as if it really was night. Also, it made it almost impossible to see what was down the corridor.

"Get back inside." He heard Ashra whisper.

Elliot saw her crouching in the dark of the corridor. He closed the door just as he saw her raise her gun, and trail down the corridor. He locked and barricaded his door again, then listened. Nothing. When Ashra wanted to be silent, she made no sound; he knew that from experience. It took five minutes until he heard a slight knock at the door. He quickly pushed everything out of the way again and opened it. Ashra slipped inside.

"What did you see?" he whispered.

"Just a metal container falling down. I'm pretty sure our friend uses the whiteout but not sure if we'll have another body. I don't think he'll kill anybody. Murder leaves tracks, and if it doesn't serve his mission, he wouldn't risk it." Ashra said.

"You know how such a man thinks, don't you?" Elliot said.

"I assume he had very comparable training to mine, yes."

"So what would you do next?" Elliot asked, keeping his voice down still.

"Kill you." Ashra gave him a meaningful glare. "You clearly are the brains of the whole operation, so you would be my next target."

"Then maybe it isn't so bad I'm going back into the ruins, is it? Sounds like I'll be way safer than you here." Elliot turned to his bed, sitting down.

"You want to go alone, don't you?" Ashra asked. "Elliot, honestly I don't like the idea one bit."

"Someone needs to go. Seriously, Ashra, the situation might be worse than Boyd or anyone suspects." He knew he owed it to her to trust her and to be transparent. Yet he knew it was unfair to apply any more pressure on her.

"What do you mean by that?" Ashra asked.

"I can't see any purpose the energy serves. No machine left. It can charge and power up. So it will grow and grow and grow . . . and then what? I'm not a physicist, but even Gernsbeck agrees on it. No reactor, no matter how sophisticated, can store an unlimited amount of energy. We need to lower it or sooner or later this thing will blow up," Elliot explained, and Ashra nodded. She had suspected something like that.

"What would happen if it blew up?" Ashra asked.

"Oh, hard to say. Antarctica would probably be a dead zone, that much I can say for sure. But would it damage beyond that? A nuclear winter where so much dust is thrown into the atmosphere it actually might block out the sun for years. It might damage the tectonic plates, the atmosphere, the ability of electronic devices to work. If it's strong enough, it might blow a hole into the shell of the earth itself. If the explosion is strong enough, this might be dangerous to the world itself." Elliot exhaled. "So we need to stop it, and I can trust none of them, and I need someone back here who can make sure I still got a base to return to once I come back. Therefore, yes. I'll go alone." Elliot looked at Ashra in the dim light. She knelt in front of him and took his hands.

"Just promise me not to play the hero, okay? Don't take unnecessary risks. Just get in there, find out what you need to find

113

out, and get back here. We need to be quick on this one, Elliot. We need to be quick and hope when this beta team comes, if there actually is one, we're ready to leave and are still alive."

"Why do you think we might not be? The traitor can't kill everybody, right? I mean, we are almost thirty people . . ." Elliot said.

Ashra leaned closer, took his face in both hands and looked at him. "I want you to listen now. Boyd knows it, Miller knows it, and I know it too. Everybody else seems not to have figured it out, but I need you to know. Why is he taking away our ability to communicate? It'll lead to a rescue team coming our way sooner or later. So why did he do it? He wants us to be unable to call for help. It's the only logical solution. Of course, you're right, he can't pick us off one by one. Impossible. So there's only one solution, one answer to the question," Ashra said.

"Someone is on his way here," he said, and Ashra nodded.

"You were always so damn clever. Yes, Elliot. I think someone is coming our way and they want us to call no reinforcements when those guys arrive," Ashra said.

"Okay, so the storm is probably a good thing. Buys us time." Elliot closed his eyes and lowered his head. "As if all of this wasn't creepy and dangerous enough."

Ashra raised his head, then leaned forward and kissed him. He hadn't expected her to do that, but his body remembered that kiss and acted automatically to it, drawing her closer and passionately, returning the affection. Her arms slung around his neck, and he felt her heart beating as he pressed her slim, perfect body against his.

****

"I'll allow it, but only because I don't have a choice," Boyd said. "I understand we need to get a closer look, and I get that you don't trust any of my men."

Elliot stood in Boyd's self-declared office and gave him a grateful nod. "Thanks, Boyd. So I need someone to get me down there. I would like Miller to do that. He can use a snowcat, and he was with Ashra when it all happened," Elliot said.

"Good choice," Boyd said and looked at Gernsbeck, the fourth person present in the room.

"The storm is dying down, probably dissolving within the next two hours," Gustavsson said. "I'll prepare and get ready." Elliot turned and left the room. Ashra and Gernsbeck remained behind. Elliot wondered what they had to discuss with Boyd, but it was too late to be curious. As he closed the door, Jordan approached him and looked around, making sure nobody listened in.

"I need to show you something," he whispered.

"In my room?" Elliot asked. "In five minutes?"

Jordan nodded, then hurried away.

Was that how it happened? Did they play on your weakness to get close to you and then your throat was slit before you could even scream?

Elliot saw Jordan vanish into the lab. The howling from outside had been reduced to a hissing sound as wind rushed over the metal. He made his way to the equipment room. McKenzie stood at the door, her assault rifle readily hanging from her shoulder and resting in both hands. Five guards seemed excessive, but Boyd had made sure at least the equipment was secure.

"What can I do for you, Professor?" she asked.

"I need a magazine for this one." Elliot took his handgun from his pocket.

"What for?"

"I'm going down into the ruins. Alone. So I'd really like to not go in there unarmed," Elliot said.

"Did Green authorize it?"

"Sure. Shall I get him?" Elliot preferred to lie instead of explaining that Green hadn't known the gun was empty from the start. McKenzie sighed and took one of the two magazines from her own belt, handing it to Elliot.

"You know how to do that?" she asked him, but he already pulled it into the hilt.

"Regrettably, yes, I do," Elliot said and made his way to his room. At least he had a fighting chance if this turned out to be a trap. Opening the door, he found Jordan already waiting inside.

"Listen," Jordan began without hesitation, as Elliot closed the door. "One of the computers they have here had all kinds of graphic programs on it. I tried a few and managed to magnify the footage we got from the site." He turned the laptop around. "Any idea what this is?"

Elliot leaned forward and saw what the camera had recorded when it filmed inside. Moments before the connection broke off, light was reflected, broken, and rays of it seemed to be stuck between objects.

"Those are crystals, aren't they?" Elliot asked, leaning closer.

"Yes, looks like they are, and those lines of light, I think that's a laser," Jordan said.

"Data transfer by light. I heard MIT is working on it. More effective than Wi-Fi, able to send much higher volumes in shorter time." Elliot paused. "I've seen something similar once before."

"Where? I thought we're still years away from perfecting data storage in crystal structures," Jordan replied.

"We are."

"It makes sense though." Jordan turned the laptop toward him again.

"In what sense?"

"Crystal data is considered so desirable because it could actually be stored indefinitely. There's no erosion, neither to the physical storage nor the data," Jordan said. "If you wanted to run an operative system for millions of years, this is more or less the only option you would have." Jordan looked at Elliot.

"Yes, I agree." Elliot rubbed his forehead, as he sometimes did when he thought things through. It made sense in a terrible way. The Ancients had this crystal technology. They had found it, not developed it themselves. The discovery had probably given their civilization a technological boost. Maybe it had also been the beginning of their end.

"We'll have trouble interfacing with it. If it's light-based technology, we might need *years* to find out how to access it. That technology doesn't exist yet," Jordan said.

"Good. Very good, actually," Elliot said. "I'm not sure we're ready to solve all their mysteries."

"Well, it also means whatever we need to do to shut it down, we can't do," Jordan said.

"What happens when we disable the operating system?" Elliot asked.

"Usually, a computer stops working and the system shuts down, but in this case? Who knows? We don't even know what it does." Jordan shrugged. "Risky move, I'd say. We should keep that as a last resort."

"Understood." Elliot nodded. "In that case, I'll try not to break anything." He gave Jordan a smile; he didn't seem to be here to kill him. He had offered him the perfect opportunity. At least one of them he could half trust. Of course, he couldn't rule out this was some sort of distraction, but he doubted it.

"I need to get ready," Elliot said.

"Good luck," Jordan replied, and got up to leave.

****

"You hear me? Please confirm with a clear copy." Boyd's voice came through the radio integrated into the orange suit Miller helped him get into. An overall made of one piece, consisting of orange rubber. The gloves were of the same material, but black. As he got into them, Miller sealed them with tape he put around his wrists. The same happened with his boots. He was wearing the winter boots as the rubber ones would cool out too quickly. Miller finally attached the handgun with a strip of tape to his chest.

"Copy," Elliot said into the radio.

Miller used the tape to attach the small camera to his helmet.

"We'll hear you until you reach the inner ring we assume," came Ashra's voice.

"We need to get you into the snowcat quickly, and same goes for the entrance. This suit is heated, but it won't help you for long in that kind of cold," Miller explained. "In your backpack is an additional battery. Keep it as a reserve because when you need to be picked up you need to call us over short-range radio. We have a signal booster integrated into the suit and a second one to a walkie-talkie in your backpack. So you should be able to contact us anyway. In case that is impossible, we'll leave a full snow gear at the entrance." Miller kept on explaining.

"Understood." Elliot said.

"You have two flashlights, a med-kit, an additional magazine, and a knife in the backpack. Just in case, we put water and rations for a day into it too. On your arm you have the map of the place." Miller pointed at the map, shrink wrapped and secured by tape. He had studied it, but a backup always made sense in case he had to find an alternative way.

"Any advice on our situation, Professor? I guess you shared your suspicions with Ashra, but I would be grateful for any pointers," Miller wrapped the winter jacket around him.

"I have no suspects to offer, Captain, sorry. But he'll wait for now, if you ask me. We're too watchful. Try to think like him. If he needs to act, he'll take risks," Elliot said. "And let Ashra do her job. She knows how these people think; she'll be the one to find him, if anyone will." Elliot looked at the captain through the plastic window in front of his face. He heard his own breathing in that suit. A small ventilation system was integrated with air filters, but he had turned it to minimum. Miller put his backpack on. Elliot tried to nod, realizing he was unable to in his suit.

"Elliot?" Ashra was on the radio. "You promise me something."

"I'll be careful. Don't you forget to be the same." Elliot replied.

119

"Miller to Base. We're moving to the snowcat now," he said.

"Affirmative," Boyd replied. Elliot turned sideways and saw Miller opening the ramp of the small garage that was attached to the equipment room. Outside, the wind howled, and snow blew into the room. Elliot tried to remind himself that a storm was nothing more than bad weather; but it wasn't completely gone yet.

"Let's go!" Miller said and went out first. Elliot followed him, his steps were slower in this new suit.

Chapter 10

Ashra remained in the control room, which was actually the lab now repurposed to serve as the new radio station; she watched them all. Gernsbeck was at his laptop, still staring at the small white ant in the vial. It was slow now, probably dying. Jordan sat next to Boyd, in front of the short-range radio. Gustavsson sat in the corner, looking at his own laptop where a geo-thermal map was visible. Clouds wandered over the area he was observing. McKenzie stood next to the door, as if to control any person leaving or coming.

If someone wanted to keep them from finding out what these ruins meant, they hadn't acted to keep Elliot away from them. So, either they were sure that Elliot would fail, or they hadn't had an opportunity. Perhaps, because they always moved in pairs, they hadn't had a chance.

"I want to go outside," Ashra said.

"Why?" Boyd asked.

"Because the backup radio has been taken, and that means the traitor must have been hiding it somewhere. Where? The snow was probably the only place available on short notice," Ashra explained.

"McKenzie? Get Roberts to accompany her," Boyd said.

"I don't know Roberts," Ashra said. "I'd prefer to go alone."

Boyd looked at her for a moment, then finally acquiesced. "You'll miss your boyfriend heroically entering the ruins."

"I think he'd understand," Ashra said. McKenzie seemed to assess her for a moment; gripping the submachine gun in both hands. An MP-5, Ashra realized. McKenzie stepped aside as Ashra stared squarely at her.

"Still angry I was too fast for you?" Ashra asked.

"Won't happen again, girl," McKenzie replied.

"We shall see," Ashra said, then left through the door.

Outside, Pierce passed her, along with two soldiers leading him to the mess. He threw her an accusatory look. Ashra had practically told Boyd that Pierce had betrayed him, and those handcuffs were probably his way of thanking him. They vanished into mess, and Ashra went in the opposite direction, heading to the south exit.

She put on one of the white winter jackets and a ski mask, pulling the hood over her head. She grabbed her pistol and removed the silencer to make it smaller. She pushed it into the pocket of the jacket, where she would be able to draw it much easier. Putting on her gloves, she opened the door.

The wind was sharp; it cut into her face. Wind brings death, her grandma always said. It chills your skin; makes your body temperature plummet if you aren't careful.

Ashra stepped outside and scanned her surroundings. The wreckage of the helicopter lay nearby, and the wind was sending waves of snow over the plain, limiting the sight of the patrols—which was why she had chosen not to wait any longer. Everyone was busy helping Elliot on his mission, or guarding the equipment. Ashra started walking, making her way straight from one building, to the other; visibility was poor, you could hardly see further than a few meters. She didn't plan to go to the second building, but if anybody was watching her, she would *appear* to change buildings. Once she was sure she was out of sight, she stopped and changed course. The third building was where she wanted to go. The depot. The place nobody was allowed to enter, except Boyd and that woman, McKenzie. Ashra had discovered that she had a higher rank than any of the soldiers, but nobody seemed to take orders from her, and she didn't give any, as if she didn't belong to the team. Special forces were a man's world. Apart for a few PR stunts, she had barely seen woman serve in those units. So, what was she? The way she moved and carried her weapons seemed to indicate she had been trained heavily. Special purpose forces, she assumed. A specialist brought in to handle a specific task. One that had something to do with the depot.

Ashra passed the large antenna, which was now mostly useless, as all equipment that could access it had been destroyed. From there on, it was only about thirty-feet to the depot. The shadow of the building appeared through the snowy winds, and Ashra quickened her pace, stomping through the fresh snow that her legs sank in; almost knee deep with every step.

She arrived at the door and saw the display panel that had been attached with four screws. *Recently* attached, judging from how shiny the screws were. The door was made of metal, so she had to crack the lock. From her belt, she got the screwdrivers and went through them to see which one would fit; then she began removing the lock by loosening the screws. Carefully, she opened it and saw the wires inside. A simple magnetic combination lock. Nothing sophisticated. Obviously, Boyd had to work with what he had found on site. Ashra began working on the wiring, pulling some of the cables together while bridging some others. The light on the lower end eventually switched to green. The door gave a loud clacking sound and opened. Ashra pushed against it, revealing a small room that was stuffed with large boxes.

There was a staircase that led downwards. Ashra was sure that was where she would find whatever Boyd was hiding. She dashed down the stairs and fumbled for the light-switch. A generator was humming in the dark. The place had its own electricity, with its own power source. Ashra pulled the ski mask off her face, removed the goggles and gloves.

She switched the lights on; the room down here was much larger than the one above. Crates were lined up. Plastic boxes mostly, but also a few long black military chests. She opened one of them. Inside, she found assault rifles, type M5 with scopes and ammo. Weapons. Of course, they had brought lots of those. She searched around for anything that stood out. Then she saw it. Resting on the table in front of her, was something that didn't belong here. A suitcase, with a belt to carry it over your shoulder. It looked like a business suitcase, leatherbound with a lock at the front. Ashra put her fingers on the opening mechanism and it snapped open. She looked through the slit to make sure it wasn't wired. When she was convinced it was safe, she lifted the lid; inside were three metal canisters embedded into a metal frame. *No*—she leaned forward; it was lead, not metal. In the middle was a display panel, which wasn't activated. Three switches sat next to it. One was red, one black and the other green. A small disc was fixed beneath the switches in the lead frame.

"I would seriously advise you *not* to play with those switches," Boyd said from behind.

Ashra closed her eyes and cursed. "Silent alarm."

"The moment you opened the casing of the lock. Yes," Boyd answered. They had been silent. She hadn't heard their steps; Boyd stood there with McKenzie behind him, her submachine gun pressed against her shoulder, the barrel pointing at Ashra.

"I could shoot you for this," Boyd said.

"What is this?" Ashra asked, wanting him to confirm her fears.

"What does it look like?" Boyd snapped.

Ashra resisted the urge to grab her own gun. Boyd seemed to sense this and raised his hand. Clearly irritated with the command, McKenzie obeyed it anyway and lowered her weapon. Boyd walked over to Ashra and put his hand on the suitcase, closing it gently.

"This, Ashra, is a W825 SADM. That stands for special atomic demolition munition," Boyd explained. "It basically is a portable nuke. Tactical. It causes an explosion equal to a quarter megaton." He sneered. "Enough to blow all of us off the map if you activate it by accident."

Ashra stared at him. "What do you need a nuke for? In Antarctica?"

Boyd exhaled slowly. "I guess you've figured that one out already, haven't you?"

"To blow up the ruins," Ashra replied.

"If necessary, yes. Not only that, but also to cause enough radiation to make any exploration of its remains impossible for quite some time," Boyd said. "If that becomes necessary."

"What scenario would make it *necessary* to destroy the greatest archeological find of mankind?" Ashra asked.

"Well, if it's in danger of falling into enemy hands of course. Also, if it poses a danger we can't get under control through any other method," Boyd said. "This is a failsafe, making sure this power source doesn't turn into a doomsday machine."

"Or if it does exactly that?" Ashra said.

125

"Well, I hope the professor will bring back some insight into that."

"So you won't shoot me?"

"McKenzie will check the weapon, then you'll accompany me back to the base. Right after you hand over your weapon. I won't put you under house arrest, but from now on you'll go nowhere without one of my men following you," Boyd said. "Neither will your professor."

"I see." Ashra saw McKenzie raise her weapon again. Ashra's hand slid into her jacket and carefully pulled out her gun.

Boyd lunged at her and grabbed it, let the magazine slide out, and loaded it through to eject the bullets from the chamber. Then he threw it to the table and drew his own gun.

"McKenzie?" he said, pointing his small compact pistol at Ashra, waving it so she would step away.

Ashra did as she was signaled. McKenzie allowed her submachine gun to slide to her side, stepping forward and drawing a small handheld PDA from her belt. Ashra watched her put it to the display; it started showing different graphs.

"Functional, it seems," McKenzie reported.

"This is madness, Boyd. We have no idea what will happen if we blow that energy source up!" Ashra cried.

"It's a last resort. Nobody was ever meant to learn it was here. Only Miller, McKenzie, and I knew about it. If everything goes according to plan, your boyfriend will crack the riddle, switch this thing off, and it will be silently flown back to a US airbase where it'll be safely stowed away. If things go south, I'd like to have options," Boyd said.

126

He was clearly convinced this was the reasonable thing to do. She wasn't Elliot; she couldn't argue with people like him, make intellectually convincing arguments or trap them in their own line of thinking; making them see their mistakes. But she was almost certain, that Boyd was as dangerous as any traitor, and the ruins themselves.

"We're done here. Let's get back," Boyd put his gun away as McKenzie picked up hers again.

Ashra was done with talking. She made her way to the stairs.

****

The wind had died down considerably as they left the depot. The other two bases were visible as they stepped out. Boyd took lead, with McKenzie staying right behind Ashra. Ashra put her hands into her jacket, with her head lowered to minimize the wind-chill. Ashra stopped. Something wasn't right.

"What?" McKenzie asked from behind. "Keep on moving."

Ashra raised her hand. Boyd stopped too.

"Keep on—" McKenzie began.

"Shut up!" Ashra yelled, and she saw Boyd raise his hand to silence the soldier.

"What is it, Ashra?" he asked. There was a sound. Barely there, but she heard it. Rattling. There was a rattling sound.

"Give me your binoculars," Ashra said to McKenzie, who refused.

"Do it!" Boyd ordered, and with a deep sigh, McKenzie took them from her belt and handed them to Ashra. It was one of those small but powerful magnifiers. Digital. Ashra looked through

127

them. She scanned the horizon. Then she saw it. A cloud of snow was the first thing she noticed; she turned the wheel, magnifying the cloud even more.

A tracked vehicle, white and long, which looked like the love-child of a snowcat and a van. No, there were two. They had used the snowstorm to approach, the clouds and snowdrifts obfuscating it from any satellite images.

"Sound the alarm!" Ashra cried. "Sound the alarm!" Boyd shook his head, then started running to the main base, grabbing his radio from his belt.

"Captain, red alert, red alert, we have incomings!" he yelled; Ashra followed him, hearing the stomping sounds of McKenzie behind her.

She had been right. The traitor had taken their chance to call for reinforcements, preparing an attack.

Chapter 11

Elliot stepped into the entrance, and he felt the cold that had crawled into the rubber suit vanish right away. He checked his PDA; sixteen degrees Celsius, it said. Sixty-one Fahrenheit. The ruins were heating up. Water dripped from the ceiling, making it slippery underfoot. If the heat was an indicator of the rising energy level, they were running out of time.

"It's warm. Sixty-one degrees Fahrenheit," he said into the radio. "The steam that was here before has almost dissolved. I'm making my way into the ruins."

"Okay, we read you loud and clear." That was Gernsbeck.

"Where's Boyd?" Elliot asked, feeling like the suit was more of an obstacle than protection.

"He went out with the lady soldier. Ashra left earlier. No idea what important stuff they have to do. It's only us now. Jordan, Gustavsson, and me," Gernsbeck answered.

"Okay. You're recording this, aren't you?" Elliot asked. "I'm switching on my camera now." Elliot touched the camera, and through his rubber gloves he felt almost nothing. He hoped this had worked.

Stepping onto the platform above the domes, he looked up to the energy source and shielded his eyes with his hand. The brilliant white ball was up there, pulsating, the moving curved beams around it now completely engulfed by it, but still moving. They were much faster now.

"It's grown, the energy source. Considerably. I would say twenty-percent at least," Elliot said.

"Is it doing anything?" Gernsbeck asked.

"Just shining brightly, like a second sun." He had to wipe water off his visor. It was raining inside the cave. "The water is melting much faster now. It's raining in here."

"Is that a problem?" Gernsbeck asked.

"No, but it might become one, if we don't move quickly. The ground is quite slippery, but I see . . ." Elliot looked into the place that made no sense and followed no principle or order. Water was now floating around them.

"Okay, to your left are those stairs that lead to the next level," Gernsbeck said, and Elliot looked to the side. He began to walk up the stairs, taking large steps to counter the unusual depth of the steps.

"Everything is made of the same white stone. As if they had it in abundance." Elliot looked at the walls, water was now flowing down and revealing a blueish icy mass behind them. Soon, the entire facility would be revealed, freed from the ice.

"Yeah, would be nice if we could send that sample to some lab." Gernsbeck sighed over the radio. There were crackling sounds in the transmission.

"Let's concentrate on the task at hand." Elliot kept on climbing up until he passed a triangular gate and stepped onto another platform. The smooth surface was free of ice, and from here he could see the entire city. It spread beyond the pillar that had blocked his view before. It spread in all directions.

"You need to find the next stairs and keep on going up," Gernsbeck said. Then there were sounds in the background. It was Boyd's voice.

"End the transmission, right away!" he yelled.

Elliot stopped. He wanted to push the button deeper into his ear to hear better, but the suit didn't allow it. There was a discussion, then the radio went silent. Something was happening at the base. Had they found the traitor? Or maybe they had another problem? Ashra maybe? Elliot closed his eyes. He knew he had to focus now. Being in a nineteen-million-year-old ruin meant that everything here could be unstable, dangerous, and potentially deadly.

As if he needed any proof, a large block of stone crashed onto the platform, and he went to one knee, shielding himself. He looked up and saw the melting ice and water rushing down.

"Main base, do you copy? Gernsbeck? Are you there?" There was no answer. Only silence. His eyes snapped open, and he forced himself to his feet. There was another line of white stairs on the platform he was on, this time much steeper. Elliot wondered what kind of species had once walked these stairs. What kind of creature had inhabited this place? He might never know. The one thing he hadn't seen, were any kind of depictions of events or persons. There was no sign of art whatsoever. It was entirely possible that smaller structures had been destroyed, of course. Maybe once, these walls had been covered with plates that had been crushed by the ice millions of years ago. There was no way to tell, really. Elliot began his next ascent, feeling his steps already getting heavy. The suit didn't make climbing stairs any easier.

On his visor, he saw a small white ant crawl. He stopped and watched it, looking down at himself. Several of them were clearly visible on the orange background. They were looking for weaknesses in the structure to reach what was below. They wanted their sample. Elliot wiped them off and began to accelerate his steps, which was even more exhausting. Finally, he reached the next level with another triangular gate, this time it led to a long bridge. It had no supporting beams but led over to another platform, that looked like a shiny, white shield rammed into the wall.

Elliot's heart began to thud. The bridge might collapse under his weight at the first step. He looked down and cursed his own foolish bravery. There was easily three-hundred-feet to the ground. What choice did he have? He had brought no climbing gear, because in the suit it would be next to impossible to use. All he could do was pray and walk. Without any railing, he stayed in the center of the nine-feet wide bridge and took his first step. The bridge held. It was made of thin stone, no thicker than an inch, yet it held. He quickly stepped over to the other side and leaned against the wall there. The path here was narrow, and one slip would be his death. Yet the bridge had been perfectly functional. After millions of years, that was a miracle in itself.

Elliot exhaled and took off his backpack; knowing getting it back on would be a pain. With sidesteps, he made his way around a corner then lunged onto the giant platform awaiting him there. He collapsed to his knees and allowed himself to breathe. He looked around, then slowly his gaze rose. In front of him, was a wall that displayed what looked like the remains of a giant relief. It was a single picture that rose from the ground, and all the way up, sixty-feet-high. Most of it had been smoothed away by the ice that had once covered the wall. Yet, he could still make out a roughly humanoid form, with kinked legs, like a goat's. There was a second creature, of which not much was left. Elliot believed he could see at least three legs though, which still remained roughly visible. Had the two been fighting? It was entirely possible this was some sort of depiction of a heroic act.

Elliot allowed the camera to record the remains of this only piece of art, then pushed himself to his feet. Looking up, he saw he had got a lot closer to the core. Twenty-two degrees Celsius, the PDA showed. Elliot opened the map to see where he had to go next. There was meant to be an opening somewhere, leading into a corridor free of ice. He scanned the wall and saw it. It was narrow, so he decided against putting his backpack on again.

His steps were now heavy, and he heard his own breath becoming labored in the helmet of the hazmat suit. Forcing himself forward, he went sideways through the entrance and stood in a broad corridor. He stopped as he realized there were two large shafts in front of him. Both seemed to be entirely empty and leading downwards into an impenetrable darkness.

Elevator shafts? They almost looked like they might have been elevators, or something comparable. Elliot blinked, as if he wanted reality to confirm what he was seeing. What were the chances the inhabitants of this place had something so comparable to the technology of modern humans?

He would later analyze the camera feed. Now, he had to keep pushing forward. He had to reach the chamber and learn more about the energy source. It was his only chance to do so.

The corridor was mostly dark; he got out his flashlights and ignited them. Immediately he saw something wasn't right. The floor was moving. In the darkness, millions of small white bodies covered the entire corridor, as if hiding from the merciless light of their second sun. Elliot looked down as much as the suit allowed. The ground he stood on wasn't covered by the small machines. He was in the part of the corridor on which the light from outside was shining. Were they hiding from the light? The ones he had encountered before didn't. Elliot turned back to the corridor, and wherever his light hit the ground, it seemed to make them part, shying away from the beam of his small flashlight. There had to be millions of them. They crawled not only on the floor, but as he waved the flashlight around, he saw they covered the walls and ceiling too. Elliot wondered if his suit would be able to withstand the sheer number of creatures if they attacked them.

Frustrated, Elliot fell to one knee again and opened the backpack. Miller had walked him through what was in it, but he hoped there was something else that could help. He pulled the med-kit aside, the battery and extra flashlight. One thing he had that Miller hadn't mentioned, were four flares. Elliot took one out and smashed it to the ground. It ignited right away. A red light filled the corridor. Raising it toward the darkness, he saw the small machines didn't react to that one. He held the flame to the ground; the machines curled together and grew dark as the flare roasted them. Elliot cursed. There were too many to be burned by his small number of flares.

He decided he had to simply try it. Either that, or he would need to turn around. Those small machines hadn't been hostile so far. They attacked to take samples, but had shown no tendency to attack him. Elliot grabbed his backpack, put everything inside again, and pressed it to his chest. Taking one deep breath, he stepped to the very edge of the corridor and looked down. His flashlight cast over the exit, and was canceled out by the bright, white light which shone through it, the source roughly a thousand feet away.

He began to run. As fast as the suit allowed him, he dashed forward. The suit made it impossible to look down at his own legs, but he assumed at least some of them were climbing up him. As he continued, some of the small, white ants crawled across his visor. These were slightly larger and easier to see than the first ones he had encountered. The few became many, and soon they covered the entire viewing field, blocking his sight. He activated his flashlights once more and pointed them into his face. The small machines shied away from the light right away. He could see he was halfway to the exit; he felt as if he was running on fumes. The machines behaved like a swarm, rushing to their target all at once. His steps grew slower. Elliot was now covered by millions and millions of the tiny machines, as if they were trying to drown him— which was probably exactly what they were trying to do. The suit was all that kept him alive now. These machines weren't harmless drones. They behaved like a pack of miniature predators. Coordinated, angry . . . aggressive.

Elliot stumbled and fell to the ground, his flashlight rolling away. As he tried to get up, he felt the weight of the millions of machines on him. If he stayed here, he would die—Elliot knew he would. They would get through the suit, and if not through the rubber, then through the tape that covered the gloves or the leather of his boots.

Setting his hand down, he crawled forward, pulled himself up again, slowly coming back to his feet; he staggered forward. The light was getting closer—now the only thing that could save him.

Gasping through the pain, he pushed one leg in front of the other. Sweat dripped down his face. His vision was completely blocked, and he had lost his backpack; it lay somewhere behind him, covered in these tiny things that were probably disassembling it right now to create more of themselves—like they would do with him if he didn't reach the light.

He wiped the visor clean, and it gave him a moment of clarity. Then somehow, he found the strength to run. Stretching himself, leaping forward, he reached the light finally and fell to the ground.

The small machines vanished almost immediately.

Elliot lay next to the exit from the corridor and breathed. The suit made it difficult, as the air filter only allowed a certain amount of air to enter. It had held against the machines though. They hadn't entered the suit. He pushed himself up, every muscle of his body aching now. He would need to find a different path back, he realized. Maybe on the lower levels. There were bridges. If he had to walk through this corridor again, the gauntlet would be his end.

Elliot looked to the left and saw the next stairs. Those would lead him all the way up to the giant platform that was connected via an equally enormous bridge to the gargantuan pillar in the center of the ruins. No more corridors between him and the mysterious room full of crystals that would hopefully bring him answers.

First, he had to do one more thing. He took the little red box from his belt—one of the few items he had left—and turned to the dark tunnel. Opening it, he removed his new tweezers then a vial. He fell to one knee, and opened the vial with a popping sound of the rubber seal. He held it into the darkness and attached the seal. Slowly, he withdrew; seeing his hand covered in the small machines. These were more grayish than their snow-white counterparts. A different breed of nanomachines, obviously. Maybe the soldiers of their caste system, like ants, had soldiers too. The vial was filled with dozens of the small machines and they all began to scurry around as he put them into the sun, desperately trying to hide from it. Elliot put them into the box and closed it. In there, they could enjoy their darkness until he put them under a microscope. He attached the box to his belt again and finally turned to the exit.

Chapter 12

The blinds of the windows—where no soldiers were positioned—were all closed. Inside the base, panicked soldiers ran through the corridors. Miller stood in the corner and yelled orders.

"Cover the south windows with snipers and close all entrances. Seal them if possible. Group Two does ammo runs; Group One takes positions!"

His men knew what to do. McKenzie passed Miller with two assault rifles, and he snatched one from her hands. She glared at him, but Miller ignored her. Instead, he threw the rifle to Ashra and winked at her.

"I assume you know how to use one of those."

Ashra only nodded, then stormed into the mess where four soldiers had taken position at the windows, aiming at the approaching fleet of tracked vehicles. Ashra took the only window not yet occupied, opened the blinds, and checked the magazine of her M5 assault rifle. Then she loaded the weapon and positioned herself next to the window.

"Russians," Boyd declared. "Those are Russian troops."

"Damnit," Miller said.

She knew what that meant. Trained in Siberia and the Ural Mountains, Russian special forces were well adjusted to snow and cold.

"Contaaaaaaact!" Ashra heard one of the soldiers scream. At the same moment, everybody but her began to fire their weapons.

A moment later, windows shattered into pieces and freezing wind entered, accompanied by bullets spraying the furniture and wooden panels that covered the walls. Ashra felt the heat as a bullet flew straight through the wall she had taken cover behind. The shot had missed her head by an inch, and she threw herself to her knees. Next to her a man was tossed back against the wall, and with lifeless eyes slid down, leaving a trail of blood.

Taking a deep breath, Ashra fought for clarity. Clarity was everything in situations like these. Ashra had been trained in combat, but she had never been at war. A spy wasn't a soldier. She had passed through dangerous territory and had seen her fair share in fire fights, but all she ever did was withdraw safely. This was something else entirely. It was a battle for dominion over territory. A scale model of war, really. Two parties, both armed to the best of their abilities, fighting each other. Their goal was the same. The annihilation of the other side, to establish permanent dominance. The path to this goal was equally clear—Kill as many of your enemies as fast as possible. It was a completely new experience for her. She lurked beside a broken window, pulled the rifle up, and aimed, seeing through the scope the enemies lining up their tracked vehicles, using them as cover—soldiers in white winter jackets and body armor poured out of them. It had to be way more troops than they had.

A shot hit the window frame; Ashra saw the man lying on top of one of the large boxes, on the back of one of the vehicles. He reloaded his rifle while keeping her in sight through his scope. Ashra took aim—not like a soldier, but like a hunter going for their prey. She knew she had only one shot. She took it.

Her finger squeezed the trigger and she was surprised how easy and familiar it felt. The bullet ripped half the man's head off and his body lost all tension. Ashra withdrew right away, and the impact of a dozen bullets made a deafening sound, as they hit the wall she was leaning against.

"RPG!" She heard one of the soldiers yelling over the noise of the firefight. RPG stood for rocket propelled grenades. She wondered if that meant they had one, or if the enemy did? The soldier threw himself to the ground and covered his ears, which probably answered her question. Ashra did the same, and what remained of the glass in the windows shattered, as blinds were torn off and the explosion sent its shockwave inside; throwing the third soldier still alive off his feet.

With blurred vision and stinging eyes, she got up just as another explosion from outside sent debris hurling towards her. Ashra pushed herself against the wall again; she knew they needed to keep on fighting. She craned her head around the corner. One of the vehicles was burning, with wounded soldiers crawling away and corpses collapsing out of the cabin and falling to the floor. Half a dozen of the soldiers were now approaching, their guns raised and constantly giving short bursts of fire as they came closer to the main base. Ashra raised her rifle and pulled the lever from single shot to burst.

"Six on five, approaching!" she yelled, and fired the first burst. It ripped through the foremost soldier and even tore the man behind him off his feet. The others spread right away, pulling their rifles up and returning fire. They all were wearing variations of AK-47 rifles. The famous Kalashnikov. Seeing the weapon confirmed her suspicion—they were indeed Russians.

Ashra took cover as another soldier began firing at them. After a few bursts, there was only silence. Both sides ceased. The Russians had lined up their armored transports to take cover behind them; they had lost at least two men and had to spare ammo.

"Americans." The voice came from the vehicles outside. Ashra saw Boyd appear, his handgun in his hand, and he pressed next to her.

"There are two simple truths here that you need to confront. The first is, that you are no heroes. No miraculous super-weapon will suddenly save you. If we continue this, we'll outnumber you seven to one, and we have heavy weapons. All of you will die." He made a dramatic pause. "Second, these ruins don't belong to you. They belong to nobody, and therefore to everybody. You don't give up if you leave them to us. You simply let us have our turn. A matter of the weaker leaving the best spot to the strongest," the man yelled.

"Idiot," Boyd hissed.

"How bad is it?" Ashra asked while dragging her magazine from the assault rifle to check it. She had about half the magazine left.

"We lost four, which means we lost about twenty percent of our men. He had about the same loss percentage wise. But that was because we took advantage of their arrival," Boyd said. "I'm no soldier, but I would say we need to have an idea and fast."

"Talk," Ashra leaned her head against the wall. "Gives us time to regroup, reload, take care of our injured, and come up with a plan."

Boyd nodded. "Okay, I'll go."

"No." Ashra grabbed his handgun and instead handed him her assault rifle. "You figure out how we deal with this. I mean, I bet you want to blow all of us up right now, but as these guys are between the depot and us, you should actually look for a method for how we can survive this," Ashra hissed at him.

"Hey, Russian! This is Ashra Shah from the Nepalese Investigation Bureau. I would like to parley!" she shouted. "Maybe we can find a solution we all are happy with so nobody else needs to die?"

There was a long pause, then the answer came with a strong Russian accent.

"I'd say we can meet in the middle!" the man yelled.

"Good. Gimme three." Ashra returned and turned to the last standing soldier. Pierce and another entered, to take the position of the fallen. Apparently, Pierce had been given his weapons back. "You guys make sure that if he kills me, he doesn't make it back to his people, hear me?" Ashra put the rifle into the back of her belt.

"Affirmative, ma'am," Pierce answered, and Ashra nodded as another soldier threw a winter jacket over to her.

"You know when I suggested this to Green, I was sure I would one day regret it. I was wrong," Ashra said as she closed the jacket, then got her gun and put it into her pocket. "I'm already regretting it."

****

She jumped out of the window, pushed her hands into her pockets, and saw that between the armored vehicles, a man in a similar white jacket to hers approached. With her hand around the handgun, she made her way to the point where the two would inevitably meet in the middle of the battlefield.

As she got closer, she saw the man was wearing oversized, black sunglasses, specially made for snow environments. He was probably in his fifties, but in excellent shape.

"My name is Fjodor Gravisloski, and I'm a colonel of the Russian armed forces," the man said.

"Ashra Shah, spy from Nepal and most unlucky woman in the world." She scowled.

"Did they send you because they thought an attractive woman would soften me up? Did you bring a bottle of vodka too?" The man laughed and passed her, looking at the base. The red metal shell around it was now covered with bullet holes.

"No, would that work? Because I could go back and see what we got . . ." Ashra replied.

"Oh, you've humor. Good. I hope you'll see the irony of it then. I bet your men are aiming at me right now. Head and heart, hmmm? My men are aiming at you. So we stand here, both so close to death and yet so brave. Like in one of these old American spy movies, with that superspy . . ." He laughed.

"British," she said.

"Pardon?"

"Those spy flicks you're referring to, they are actually British," Ashra said.

"Oh, you do have a sense of humor. Surprising for one so young to be so calm in the face of death," the colonel said.

"I haven't even been shot at right now, so I consider this the safest spot I've been in the last fifteen minutes. So shall we get this over with?"

"Sure. Your men will lay down their weapons and leave the base, and in return I'll spare their lives. You have my word. None of them will be harmed in any way, and they will be released once we're done here," the colonel said.

"Oh, if it was up to me, you could have those damn rocks out there and I would leave. Problem is, these guys are as stubborn as you are, and they have their orders," Ashra said.

"You would leave? Ashra Shah? Professor Elliot Brand's girlfriend, right?" The colonel smiled.

Ashra smiled back. This man was a soldier, but in the art of espionage, he was a terrible amateur. He knew this from an inside source. The traitor had told him. He had just given that away.

"Elliot is neither a fanatic nor a martyr, so why should *I* be one?" Ashra asked. "Has your little bird told you what it is we found?"

"A seemingly unlimited power source buried in a ruin so old it shouldn't exist at all. Am I about right?"

Ashra nodded. "It's a bit too big to be transported away though. You would have to study it on site. How is that going to work? If you kill us, our replacements will show up in a few days. More soldiers. A battalion probably. They're going to do to you what you did to us. Are you authorized to start World War three, Colonel?"

"Are you?"

"No, but we didn't start shooting," Ashra said.

"You've broken international law by bringing armed forces to Antarctica. We only moved to uphold law," the colonel said.

"You could have called UN." Ashra shrugged. "Listen, those guys aren't idiots. We're prepared for you winning the battle.

They prepared for everything. So there's no scenario in which you win." Ashra stepped closer.

"Ms. Shah, I have my orders, and even if I stood no chance to fulfill them, I would look for a way to do so anyway. I'm a soldier; I follow my orders. My orders are to take control of this facility. So that's what I'll do." He stared at her. "You aren't even American. We have no quarrel with your government."

"I kinda got caught in the middle, you know?" She smiled.

"Tell the commander in there what I offer. You have ten minutes. Then we'll start to get serious," the colonel said. "So try to convince him. Nobody needs to die!"

"I'll deliver your message." Ashra turned around. Holding her breath, she started walking back to the base. When she looked over her shoulder, she saw him still standing there, as if he wanted to prove that he didn't fear them. She didn't stop walking though. The door at the side of the building opened, and Miller knelt there, his rifle pointed at the other side. Quickly, she stepped inside, and the door was closed.

"So, what did he say?" Boyd asked, sitting on the floor.

"He was winning time, just like I did. Prepare your men; they're coming," Ashra said to Boyd, and Miller handed her another assault rifle and a belt with two magazines.

"Good, because we have a plan." Boyd smiled at her.

Chapter 13

Elliot had to shield his eyes, and it almost felt as if the light was managing to pierce his suit, flesh, and bones to shine him to death. Gasping, he stepped over the giant platform that extended from the cave wall and led to the large, rounded bridge, leading all the way to the white ball of energy pulsating there. He realized he should burn. So close to the thing, he should burn to cinders, yet he felt it wasn't considerably warmer down here. The energy source should have burned the ice away like a flame thrower.

Something kept the temperature under control. No, it wasn't the energy heating this place up. It was the engine. It was so hot, the air around the pillar began to flicker. Elliot realized it was overheating. He went into a crouching position and touched the stone he stood on. It was warm. Even through the gloves he could feel its warmth. So was it the *light* these machines feared, or had they learned that the light came with the heat? Most machines, especially those that contained complicated machinery didn't behave well in heat.

How hot could the machine that ran this place get before it broke? What would happen if it did? Elliot had the feeling they wouldn't like to find out.

Looking to the ground and putting his hand up again, Elliot felt he was suddenly in a hurry. Carefully, he stepped on the bridge, which was another large, elegant arch, leading from his platform to a ring around the pillar. The stone was so thin he was surprised it didn't crumble away once he stepped on it. But it didn't. He forced himself forward, the bright light now almost engulfing him. There was a deep howling of the rounded beams, still rotating

145

inside the energy source. The glare was so intense he could barely look at it, but he still saw them turn around a virtual center.

He saw the stairs going downwards and upwards from the ring, and he closed his eyes. Even through his eyelids, he saw the light. Without goggles, which he couldn't put on because the helmet didn't allow him to, it was impossible to see in the intensity.

His hand finally touched the pillar, and he felt his steps grow less secure. He had to take stairs, and in his blinded state, that would be a problem. There were still no railings at all. If he slipped, he would go all the way down, and he had no security rope or anything that could save him.

He pressed himself against the pillar and started inching down the stairs. A thought occurred to him. *How long could he stare into a light so bright it broke through his eyelids before it did permanent damage?* If this left him permanently blind, or even blind for an extended amount of time, he was dead. It made him move slightly faster. His feet found the edge of a stair and slid down; he took a few more steps and repeated the same with the next. Step by step he descended, until he suddenly felt no more wall to his left. He was at the entrance. Pulling himself inside, he opened his eyes.

All he saw was white for a moment, before his view gradually returned, beginning at the edges of his vision. He realized he was not in the dark. The light here was blue. Breathing in sharply, he looked around; he was in a room full of blue crystals. They were all glowing with a pulsating effervescence. Hundreds of beams of light spread between them, changing position and connection every few seconds... Elliot stepped forward and slowly moved his hand between two crystals that were connected by a thin, blue beam. The moment he disturbed it, the structure immediately switched, and a new path of light circled around the obstacle of his hands and connected the two points indirectly. This was a

146

machine that had been running for millions of years. A machine created from two elements neither aged nor corroded. Crystals and light. For both, millions of years were nothing. He had seen this before. A much simpler version of it. The Ancients, the civilization he had encountered under the Himalaya, had a crystal to store information, too. It had been lost when the caves collapsed. Elliot wondered if they had adopted their technology from finding a room like this? Possibly, considering how similar their single crystal cube worked and how this was set up. This here was way more sophisticated. This wasn't a hard drive; this was a machine.

Elliot had to laugh; he remembered his speech he always gave about how humanity would leave nothing lasting beyond two-hundred and fifty-thousand years. It was wrong. Someone would probably find a perfectly shaped diamond and realize this form had been made using a diamond grinder. Diamonds would outlast any other sign of civilization. Just like these had.

Elliot felt a shiver go through him, despite the warmth in there. This was the oldest machine on the planet, and it wasn't some wheel or something primitive. The oldest machine on planet earth seemed to be . . . a computer. An advanced computer, in fact. No doubt storing data beyond all comprehension

Elliot waved his camera attached to his helmet around, but when he looked aside, he saw the ants had almost completely eaten it. He hoped the hard drive inside was still intact, at least having made a recording of the first part of his journey. As he turned, he accidentally pushed against one of the outer crystals. It made a sound, as if moving. Elliot stopped and looked around. Then he slowly grabbed it, his hand closing around the crystal. He had no idea what would happen if he removed it, but his curiosity convinced him the danger was a calculated one.

He pulled at it and the crystal moved, suddenly resting in his hands, the broad tip of it still glowing with that strange blue light. It was way more intense than his flashlight, and if nothing else would remain, this crystal would be at least evidence of what he had encountered. Pushing it into the bag at his belt, he sighed. Time. Time was running out. The battery of the suit was limited and so was his time to explore. Yet, there was one final place he needed to go. At the far end of the oval room was another exit. A narrow gate like all the others he had seen. Only this one led into the pillar. Finally, he would get to see what this place was about. It was why he had come here.

****

There was a slight pull. He felt as if he was being pulled into the center of the pillar as he stepped through the opening on the wall. The magnetic field, not at full strength, was present there.

He followed the pull and stepped onto a ring-shaped ledge that went all around the inner hollow tube that rested in the center of the pillar. In the middle was a giant, black tube, that seemed to be made out of some kind of metal. Around it, curved beams made of the same black metal rotated. It looked almost as if the material was absorbing light. It seemed featureless and obsidian, with no reflection. The crystal gave no light to see with, as he stepped to the edge of the four- feet wide ledge. He looked down and saw the tube vanish into darkness. The heat here was unbearable and his ventilation system was running on overdrive. It was the center of the place, and whatever this machine was, transported the energy from below where it was harvested up to the pulsating core above.

The walls were moving. Elliot saw millions, if not billions, of the white ants running in circles in the same direction as the beams. In a spiral movement, they ascended the pillar. Elliot stared at them; they were almost hypnotic. They didn't descend off the walls and attack him. Instead, they made circles upwards. Silently fulfilling whatever purpose they had.

Elliot knew that he would never understand this machine. He hadn't the first idea about reactor technology. Archeology usually doesn't need that specific expertise. Nothing that had energy like this had ever fallen into the realm of archeology. Everybody thought he might be the most qualified to investigate this place, but the truth was, he was no more qualified than any of the others. Maybe even less. Ashra or Miller would have been better at the whole physical part of this exercise. He should have sent them. At least he knew that neither of those two were the traitor. Instead, he had gone himself, eager to see all of this with his own eyes. Technology left behind by some ancient species unknown to man, but ruling the earth millions of years before him. Oh, what a find. It had been vanity, if he was honest. He regretted it now. The problem was, it was too late for regrets. It was too late to change the decisions he had already made. With a sigh, he turned and left the inner machine. It was even hard to step outside the room, with every bit of metal drawn to this central pillar. He wondered if this pull had brought him over the edge. Would he have fallen to the end of this tube, or would he had been glued to the central tube and starved to death there?

Outside, he passed the room full of crystals and made his way to the exit. A rumbling went through the pillar at that moment. Stopping, he listened. The sound of large pieces of stone shattering below could be heard. The machine seemed to be running fine. It was the pillar that lost integrity, the heat probably too much for it to take. The material was spreading, the structural integrity slowly eroding. When would it finally collapse? It was impossible to say. But what he was sure of, was that it would. At some point it would collapse. What would happen then? Elliot could almost imagine the giant ball of white, pure energy falling as the structure it was resting on collapsed. Dust would fill the entire cave. Yet, what happened to this energy if the machine providing it failed? No, he decided the more important question was what would happen if the machine containing it failed? Would it discharge? An explosion as if the entire US arsenal of nuclear warheads were exploding at one point? Elliot wished he had contact with Gernsbeck. What could an explosion like this do? Blow a hole into the atmosphere? Lead to tectonic shifts? He honestly didn't know. He had the feeling that whatever it was, wouldn't be good though. Not for those around, and probably not good for all of mankind. A nuclear winter at best—an extinction worthy event at worst.

Elliot's eyes went through the room, and he saw the crystals exchange data via light. This was the heart of this machine. If he could only understand what they were meant to say. Whatever interface had been once used with all the other controls had eroded long ago. Only the computer remained, faithfully doing whatever it was meant to do for all eternity. This had to be by design. It couldn't be a coincidence. No human computer would run indefinitely. None of them would make it to a hundred-thousand years. So creating one that did, that had the potential to do so had been a very specialized and crucial task to the Ancestors. It had been needed for some reason. But why?

To keep the reactor going?

For who or what? So it would still be there upon their return?

They had never returned. Whatever had happened to them, they were long gone. But who or what could have destroyed a species this highly developed? Who or what could possibly wipe them out, leaving these ruins empty as the snow and ice slowly claimed them? More importantly, why had the machine not been running back then? Whatever purpose it had, also probably eroded into dust millions of years ago. Only the source of energy remained.

What the hell happened here? Elliot thought, moving again to the crystals. His hand touched the light beams, and he watched them adjust to deal with the new obstacles. If only Teller could be here. His old mentor and professor might not have the right answers, but he had always been brilliant at asking the right questions. *What would he ask? What would he say?* Elliot smirked, because he knew the answer.

"Bring the events you know into sequence. Track the steps of history by making a map, then fill the gaps." His voice seemed to echo in Elliot's head. He smiled. It felt comfortable.

"I don't have enough to work with. Not yet," Elliot answered. "But great advice."

Teller would never have allowed that excuse. "Two events are enough. All you need to do is fill a lot of gaps then," Teller whispered in his mind.

"The Ancestors built this place. A facility with giant walls and an even larger giant reactor in its center. They built it here at the pole where half the year it's dark and half the year there's sun. Then, after living here for an unknown period of time, something went wrong. They started to die, or their numbers dwindled. So they created a machine that would continue to work for all of eternity. Again, something went wrong. The place was—long after they were dead—covered by snow first, then large masses of ice moved over it, engulfing it, cutting off oxygen, and slowly running down the machine. We know it only reactivated recently. Of course, there is oxygen. A little gets through the ice, the snow. Diffusing down here. So the machine kept on running. Probably in some sort of maintenance mode. These small drones repairing it, maintaining it, keeping it brand new for millions of years." Elliot stopped. "But they didn't rule this place. No. In the darkness, those gray ones did. They came out, spread. Ate away everything they could to replicate. That is why there's no metal anymore of any kind. Not because it rusted. Frozen things don't do that. They were *consumed* in the darkness by the gray ants." Elliot remembered the map. Below this place are thousands of tunnels, so far unreachable. An entire system. How many of these could be down there? Billions?

"No, they existed before, didn't they? They were your undoing. Maybe you lost control? Maybe someone used them against you? The creation that had maintained this place suddenly turned on you." Shaking his head at the thought of an entire species suddenly turning on their masters and devouring them was haunting. "Then the glacier broke, and the reaction driving this machine finally got what it needed most. Oxygen. As much oxygen as it needed. So it began charging. But why? What's its purpose?" Elliot closed his eyes.

He had to go. He knew he was losing valuable time, and whatever this mystery was, he wouldn't share what he had found if he died down here. Making sure the crystal was at his side, Elliot took off his helmet and tied a scarf over his eyes. Then he put it on again, sealed it, and made his way to the stairs. He assumed the blind ascent would be harder than going down had been; but at least he had a source of light strong enough to pass the corridors this time. He hoped it worked—or he would expire in that dark, cursed tunnel.

Chapter 14

"They have taken up position between us and Base Two," Boyd whispered, as if he was afraid the Russians could hear him from the mess. "We had five men there who they all killed. I'm guessing there are sixty of them left. Enough to deal with us, but as they consider Base Two empty, they're now besieging us."

"I wonder what they're waiting for?" Ashra asked.

"On us to make a mistake. They know storming a place full of soldiers is a death trap. So they're waiting for an opening. Patiently," Boyd whispered.

"Which will be their undoing," Miller said.

Ashra raised her brows. "Will it?"

"The storm." Boyd sighed. "It seems to be turning. It's coming back. Not as bad as before, but without shelter, they'll freeze to death. They have to withdraw to Base Two."

"No, they'll attack before that happens," Ashra said.

"Which is why we get them first." Boyd dragged her away from the window. All three of them crouched on the floor.

"There's a passage between this station and the Base Two. It's an underground tunnel, running between the two stations. We store food down there, some heavy equipment for the drilling usually done here," Miller said. "Gernsbeck pointed it out. The entrance is right down there in the corridor."

Ashra looked at the window. "It runs right under them?"

"Yes, it does. So we could blow them up, but what we could also do is . . ." Boyd grinned.

"Get most of our guys into Base Two and attack from there," Ashra concluded, even though they were still heavily outnumbered. "Right into their backs."

"No, we don't have to do that," Miller said. "We wait until the storm hits and they can't go anywhere for shelter but there. We set a trap, and either they give up or we kill them all."

Ashra didn't like the idea of a slaughter, but she wasn't naïve about what the Russians had planned for them.

"Captain Miller?" McKenzie entered the room, ducking down and moving to their position.

"Not now, Sergeant," Boyd sighed; annoyed at the disturbance.

"No, exactly now." McKenzie insisted, and Ashra's head snapped up. Boyd looked at her, then nodded. McKenzie crawled to the corridor, and they followed her. There they all got to their feet.

"We found him a minute ago. In the bathroom," McKenzie said.

"Who?" Boyd asked.

"It's Gernsbeck, sir," McKenzie opened the door of the bathrooms. Gernsbeck lay there, leaning against the wall, his throat showing a clean cut and blood still seeping from the wound onto his clothes. Boyd entered first. He stepped over the pool of blood that was spreading on the floor and crouched next to the body. Ashra followed, leaning forward.

"Cut his throat clean, windpipe and artery with one quick cut," Ashra said.

"Why Gernsbeck?" Boyd asked.

"Because he came in. Caught him in the act," Ashra said.

"Act of what?" Boyd turned to her.

Ashra began to kick the first toilet door open. There were three of them. "Good question," she said, then went to the second. She kicked that one, and on the toilet seat she saw it—a package of C4 with a timer attached to it. It had another fifty-five seconds to go. Cursing, Ashra moved to the bomb and withdrew the cable from the tribe into the charge. The countdown stopped.

"That bastard wanted to blow us up!" Boyd hissed.

"Yes, but he hadn't thought it through," Ashra looked at the bomb. "Wait here." She stood up and went out of the restroom, going straight to the quarters right next to it. They were empty. She went to the opposite door and saw Pierce sitting there, his rifle aimed through the window outside. "Hey," Ashra greeted him. "You're back in service, hmm?"

"Yes, ma'am." He turned back to his scope, scanning the outside. "We need every gun we can get now."

"What about your friend? The other suspect?" Ashra asked.

"He was the first to go down, ma'am." Pierce looked at her once more.

"I'm sorry to hear that."

"Well, he was quite annoying," Pierce said and turned back to his mission at hand. "But a nice guy, all in all."

Ashra left the room again, closing the door.

155

Miller waited for her outside. "What are you doing?" he whispered, taking her arm.

"I'm trying to find out who the traitor is," Ashra said. "The guy who almost blew us up."

The door of the lab opened, and Jordan stepped into the corridor. Seeing two soldiers there, he quickly moved away from them. Boyd came out of the restroom.

"I need to take . . . I need to go to the restroom," Jordan explained.

"Take the ladies room; we're working inside," Ashra said, and Boyd quickly closed the door.

"Did he just try to get the bomb? Maybe he realized he made a mistake?" Boyd asked with a lowered voice.

"Or he wanted to see why it didn't explode," Ashra said. "Down the corridor. He would have survived there." Ashra looked at Miller. "Keep an eye on him." She made her way down to the door of the lab and opened it. The blinds were all closed, and it was dark inside. Jonah Gustavsson sat on the floor, his laptop on his knees. Boyd entered right after her.

"Sir, the weather front is returning. I think Professor Brand was right. The storm is attracted to the electromagnetic field. It bounces back and forth, losing speed then turning around." Gustavsson looked up.

"When will it be here?" Boyd asked.

"About an hour, I'd say. Maybe even less. Another two and it'll hit with full force. Those guys will freeze to death out there!"

Ashra looked around the lab. The computers were all on the floor now. The two men had taken cover. She stepped over to Jordan's working place. A bag of potato chips lay there, crumbs scattered all over the place and his laptop resting on the floor. She saw that the program they used to receive radio was running. There was no call history of course. Only the frequencies.

"Didn't you order a radio silence?" Ashra asked Boyd.

"I did," he said.

"We were waiting for a transmission from Professor Brand," Gustavsson explained. "He doesn't know about the Russians yet."

That was right. He didn't know. She was aware of it, too. But he also didn't know about the storm. She just hoped he was quick enough to come back first or was smart enough to stay in the entrance of the ruins.

"Did Jordan talk to anyone on the radio?" Boyd asked Gustavsson.

"Who would he talk to?".

"Morse code," Ashra said. "He could have contacted them via morse code."

Boyd nodded.

"He's under a lot of pressure! We aren't used to this, you know? Shooting and all that," Gustavsson said. "That poor guy is nervous. He went to the bathroom like five times in the last hour!"

Boyd looked at him, then back to Ashra.

"Arrest him," Ashra whispered. Boyd stormed out of the lab.

157

"Did I say something wrong?" Gustavsson asked. Ashra smiled at him. Sitting there with his glasses on, the overweight man looked so lost.

"It's all right. It's nothing you said," Ashra said. "Gernsbeck is dead."

"What? How . . . Was he shot?" Gustavsson looked around as if he expected him to meet the same fate any second.

"No. He wasn't shot," Ashra replied. As she got up, she unplugged Jordan's laptop and put it under her arm. Without another word, she walked out. She hated to leave the poor guy alone in there, but she had to make sure their plan worked. Not only did their life depend on it, but Elliot's too.

****

They opened the hatch, and Miller was the first to climb down. It was less of a tunnel, more of a cave complex below. Ashra heard the humming of the generator; it had to be down there.

Twelve of the remaining sixteen soldiers stood ready, fully armed and equipped with both assault rifles and hand grenades, prepared to climb down the stairs. Boyd stood next to Ashra.

"You're sure you want to stay?" he asked.

"We need to maintain the illusion we're still here. So yes. I'll stay here with the other four," she said.

"And the traitor and the weatherman." Boyd sighed. "He did good actually, didn't he?"

"Yes. Where's Jordan?"

"Tied and gagged in my bureau. Chained him to a pipe." Boyd reached into his pocket and took a key out, handing it to Ashra.

"Just in case you need to move him. But I don't mind if you put a bullet to his head."

"Yeah, I'll make that a spontaneous decision, I guess." She still had his laptop under her arm. Putting it aside, she looked at McKenzie who wordlessly handed her back her assault rifle. The only female soldier, McKenzie, was going to stay here with her too.

"Good luck," Ashra said, and Boyd shouldered his own gun, then slowly moved toward the hatch. "I still have your pistol,"

"Keep it. I have a replacement. If you finish him, use my gun." Boyd grinned and began his descent. When he was finally down there, she closed the hatch and sealed it again.

"You think the plan will work, ma'am?" McKenzie asked.

"Ashra. Please call me Ashra." She closed her eyes for a moment. Exhaustion was slowly kicking in. It had been days since she'd had any sleep. "And we have a reasonable chance, but it won't be pretty."

"Good." McKenzie turned and made her way back to the mess, to take her position with the other soldiers. Ashra watched her, then strolled over to Boyd's office. She opened the door and saw Jordan there, chained to the pipe at the wall just as Boyd had said. He mumbled something through his gag and pushed at his restraints. Ashra looked at him for a moment, then closed the door again. She then returned to the mess and sat next to the door.

"Report any movements," McKenzie ordered the soldiers. Pierce was among them. McKenzie was in command now. If the Russians attacked—which was possible because the wind was beginning to rise and howl and they were probably aware they were running out of time—then they stood no chance. Five against sixty wasn't a fight they could win. If they retreated to Base 2 where they were expected by men in cover, armed to their teeth and positioned in the most important strategic points, they would hopefully surrender.

"Watch out for snipers," Ashra said. "They'll make their opening move by trying to take out one of you."

This was war, and she had no desire to go to war with anyone. Part of the reason why she had always deemed her job important was because she prevented wars. She prevented terror attacks and crimes.

Chapter 15

Elliot stumbled out of the entrance and allowed himself to fall against the wall, slowly sliding down it. Gripping his helmet, he dragged it off his head and caught a breath of fresh air. The light had protected him from the gray ants, but the heat in his suit had been unbearable as he had made his way back.

He had needed a lot more time to get back than he'd originally needed to get there. Now he felt sweat running down his body. He knew that sweat kills you in the cold. He would wait for it to dry in the suit before putting on the winter clothes Miller had left for him in a large, gray backpack. He opened it. Inside was some overalls, boots, a winter jacket, and a bottle of water. He opened the water; it was partially frozen and hurt his teeth. He drank anyway. Dehydration was the other thing that got you killed in the cold. It made you tired, and when your eyes closed, the cold crawled into your body and steadily slowed you down until you never woke up—before being completely frozen. Elliot removed the pistol still attached to his chest. It looked functional. It seemed that stainless steel resisted the gray ants much better than plastic did.

Which meant this civilization had probably not had it.

He wondered how long he had. Was he wasting precious time here? How long before the pillar would break? Hours? Days? Elliot had the feeling it would be sooner rather than later.

Fighting the urge to close his eyes, he decided he was dry enough. With hasty movements he ripped off his hazmat suit and wriggled into the overalls, closing the zipper. Then he put the jacket over. There was a sharp wind passing through the valley, spreading its icy cold. It sounded like an ancient beast awakening, giving the scenery an additional creepiness, it really didn't need.

He put the gloves and ski mask on and the hood over his head. Then he grabbed the radio from the suit. He doubted it would still work, but when he pressed the receiving button, he was surprised to actually hear a crackling sound.

"Brand to Base One do you copy?" he asked, and received no answer. He waited for a long while and then repeated the process. No reply. Why should this be easy?

Elliot forced himself up and pulled the almost empty backpack on his bag. He put the pistol into the pocket of his jacket and looked down the valley. The wind would come from the front until he was out of the valley; he would take a sharp left turn to reach the base after a long walk over the plains. He wondered if he could make the walk in one long march, or if he would have to rest by the end of the valley between some rocks. There was only one way to find out. At least it was easier to walk now, without the suit. Keeping his head down, he pushed himself forward step by step.

"Stop!" a voice suddenly yelled. Elliot looked up; a soldier stood there. "Don't move!"

Elliot wondered what accent that was. Russian? He was wearing a different uniform than their soldiers. A winter suit but with spots on it. The rifle he held looked like a Kalashnikov. Exactly like the one Abas had in Afghanistan. Elliot raised his hands. A second soldier appeared from the side, now allowing his rifle to hang down as he approached.

"The gun is in my jacket," Elliot said, and the man grabbed it with a straight arm and slowly withdrew it.

The first soldier said something in Russian into a radio attached to his shoulder. A reply came also in Russian. The soldier waved with his gun—Elliot was meant to follow him. Confused; he shook his head.

"Whatever you want," he lowered his arms. What were the Russians doing here? Had they attacked the base? Was Ashra okay? He knew he would get answers to these questions at the end of their walk.

Elliot was led to the end of the valley where another two soldiers awaited them, in front of some large vehicles that looked like a mix of a tank and a snowcat. The men talked in Russian before Elliot was pushed to the large loading space in the back. The doors opened, and Elliot climbed into it with the soldier following him. At least he wasn't going to have to walk.

****

The soldier didn't say a word, and Elliot didn't engage in conversation. He took his mask off and waited patiently, as the vehicle made its way through the ice. This man wasn't the one to talk to—he was a soldier with the mission to guard him. When they finally stopped, the man drew his pistol, leaving his rifle over his shoulder, and waved to the door. It was open, and the sun broke into the dark of the windowless transport cabin. Feeling stiff now, with his muscles hurting, Elliot climbed out and saw six more of the vehicles making two lines, with soldiers behind them. In the background their base was visible. This was a siege.

A man stood outside, flanked by two soldiers. He was older; maybe fifty. "The great Professor Brand," the man said with a heavy Russian accent.

"In person," Elliot answered. "What the hell is going on here?"

163

"My name is Colonel Fjodor Gravisloski. I've seized those ruins for my country, and we are right now in the process of evacuating all unwanted elements."

Elliot stood in front of him and looked at the soldier behind the vehicles. A sharp wind hit him, and he felt the shiver run through his body. The storm was coming back.

"I assume by evacuating them, you mean in plastic bags?" Elliot asked.

"If I have to," the colonel said. "Now we have of course a much better negotiation position as we have their lead scientist."

Elliot laughed. "You didn't meet Boyd Green, did you? He doesn't care for me, I can assure you that."

"Well, maybe Ms. Shah does then?" the colonel asked.

Intimidation; the attempt to make him scared. This man had been trained in interrogation technique by someone who has seen way too many movies. Elliot decided to give him a taste of how hard he was to intimidate.

"Oh I see. May I ask you a question, Colonel?" he asked. "Are your superiors total idiots, or are you the fool who didn't get what's going on here?" He saw one of the Russians step forward, probably to hit him. The colonel raised his hand.

"You could be an American, too. So daring, Professor." The colonel laughed at him.

"Yeah, knowing one will die does that to people," Elliot said.

"Oh, we won't kill you, don't worry. We're looking forward to working with you actually. You've been designated a person of interest on this mission."

"I wasn't talking about you. There's an energy source in that ruin as you probably already know. It's got the power of . . . well, let's say your nuclear arsenal isn't that relevant anymore. This energy source is charging and charging, and it keeps on charging. You know what will happen? It'll explode. Boom." Elliot stared at him. "What does that mean? Well, let's put it like this; if there are any Russian citizens of relevance in Antarctica, it might be a good time to get them out. Not that it'll help them too much when the . . . forget it. Let me make this short. I need to go back to work to find a solution, or it doesn't matter who kills who tonight. Because in a month from now, nobody on this planet will be alive."

"A bluff," the Russian said, and Elliot saw he wasn't convinced.

"Really? You think that's the kind of story I come up with when I'm bluffing?" Elliot asked.

The colonel pressed his lips together. "So, what can we do about it?"

"Well, in there's a geophysicist. The only guy who knows something about physics that we have. I would love to ask him exactly that question," Elliot said, and he saw the Russians exchange looks. Concerned looks. "I'll take it this is no longer an option?"

"He's been killed as far as I know," the colonel said.

Elliot closed his eyes. "Brilliant." He hissed the air out. "Let me guess, that infiltrator idiot is one of yours? He actually did a great job costing us valuable time. Well, in that case, I would love to use your communications to get someone on the line who can help," Elliot said; the colonel made a strange face. "Don't tell me you don't have any long-range communications . . ."

"We're under orders to keep strict radio silence," the colonel replied.

"Are you kidding me? Have you heard a word I said?" The wind was getting colder now. It blew snow over the little plaza between the three buildings. "We need to get this under control, or we'll have bigger problems than radio silence."

"Our communications system can only reach our outpost near Concordia," the colonel said. "I'll report to them."

"Then maybe they can get . . ." Elliot stopped mid-sentence. "Colonel. I need to deal with this."

"I'm afraid I can do little for you right now. For now, we'll keep you in custody," the colonel turned to the man beside him. With their black ski masks and white jackets, these guys all looked the same, but he seemed to be some sort of second in command. "We'll evacuate now to Base Two. A storm is arriving."

"Yeah? Well, you know this machine is attracting storms here, right?" Elliot asked.

"These men will escort you there." The colonel waved his hand, and the two men flanked him, taking his arms. Elliot went with them, while the men slowly left their positions to withdraw from their vehicles.

"We don't have time for this! I need to talk to my people!" Elliot yelled, but it was too late. The colonel was already occupied with other tasks, which Elliot knew would ultimately be irrelevant. Of course, he had made the initial explosion more urgent than it probably was, but nevertheless, this miniature war in the Antarctic ice desert wasn't helping them at all.

****

166

Their rifles first, the soldiers approached the second base. Elliot was further behind with his two guards. In front of it, laid the bodies of some of the soldiers. So they had begun killing each other. He had secretly hoped this had purely been a standoff situation so far. Obviously, that wasn't the case. They had killed each other. Which probably meant this wouldn't end until one of the sides was wiped out. Considering their convoy of almost fifty soldiers was way bigger than the smaller group Boyd commanded, Elliot assumed the chances were heavily in favor of the Russians.

The first soldiers entered Base 2, and Elliot looked back to Base 1 where his people were. He had considered running, but the chance these soldiers would shoot even if they had orders not to, was simply too big. He decided to wait for his next opportunity to speak with the colonel, in the hope of convincing him this time to stand down and cooperate. Making them see reason was the only hope they had. If this cat and mouse game could play out a few more days, he was truly convinced it would all end without winners.

"Go." The soldier to his left tried to order him in English. Elliot stepped forward to enter the building. Getting out of the cold wind that announced the coming storm with its icy whispers was tempting—even if he had to be a prisoner to do so.

He entered among the last of the men; inside, a soldier passed them with an axe. The Russians were discussing in their own language and gesturing at the doors that were all locked.

Elliot blinked, and he appreciated that he hadn't been handcuffed or tied up. Maybe he should have been insulted that he wasn't considered a threat at all, the fact that they didn't restrain him. Yet Elliot didn't recall any locked doors before. He hadn't been over here before, but it was basically the same set up. A long corridor with rooms either side and a large room at the end leading to the storage area. It was quite crowded to have fifty men only in the corridor. Elliot saw concern in the eyes of the colonel. They probably had the same thought. This was perfect for a—

An eruption of noise tore him from his thoughts as the American soldiers opened fire. The thin walls were ripped apart; Elliot covered his ears. The warm blood of a Russian soldier sprayed onto his face. There was a loud bang, which Elliot just about heard over the ringing in his ears.

Elliot had never been in a firefight. His mind was still functioning enough to realize that they had run into a trap, and it wasn't meant to take prisoners. Completely lost on what to do, he did the only thing he could come up with. He threw himself to the ground, covered his head with his arms, and waited. Bodies stumbled over him. Blood pooled on the floor and he felt the warm fluid soak into his clothes. As his hearing returned, it was filled with the sound of shooting. A trap, a perfect trap had been laid. An explosion ripped through the corridor, followed by screams.

"Surrender! We surrender!" The voice of the colonel could be heard screaming between bursts.

"Gun away, hands behind your head. One false move and it won't be only you who pays with his life!" That was Miller yelling now.

"Miller!" Elliot cried and sat up. The corridor was littered with dead bodies. Some were still dying, bleeding from several wounds, coughing and spasming. It was a nightmarish field of agony and death. Over those bodies now stepped Miller, and behind him four Russians, seemingly unharmed, were kneeling, with two American soldiers keeping them in check.

"Any wounded or casualties?" Miller yelled, and nobody answered. Elliot slowly stood up.

"Professor? Looks like you came back just at the right moment." Miller smiled. Elliot needed a moment to gather himself. A soldier, gasping as blood seeped from several wounds in his torso, lay right next to him. Miller shouldered his rifle, then took out his pistol.

"Wait!" Elliot cried as the soldier held the gun to the man's head. Miller looked at him, mouth open with surprise. "I'm sure there's a law against executing a prisoner of war."

"I'm sure there is, too," Miller said. "But shall I have him suffer? That bullet's pierced his lungs. He's gonna suffocate as blood fills his lungs. Slow and painful. You think that's better?"

Elliot stared at him, then Miller smirked. He pulled the trigger. The bullet went straight into the man's head. It lolled down onto his chest, as his body slid to the ground. Elliot closed his eyes for a moment, then looked at Miller.

"Professor? Glad you're alive." Boyd greeted him, stepping over the bodies of the dead Russians. "Looks like we got that problem solved."

"Was it necessary to slaughter them?" Elliot knew they would think him to be naive for such a question.

"They wanted to do the same with us. Also we couldn't handle or control sixty of them. Now the numbers are quite more manageable." Boyd glanced at the few Russians who were left. Didn't he see that he had just killed almost fifty young men simply doing their duty? Or did they just not care?

169

"Professor, while we clean up here, I would suggest you accompany me over to the Base One," Boyd said. "We all want to hear what you encountered; I suppose."

Elliot nodded; Boyd led the way out of the corridor. Elliot felt numb as he followed him.

He almost didn't notice when the shooting began again. Doing the only trick he knew, he threw himself down right away; this time windows shattered. Some Russians had stayed outside, and those were the ones now opening fire on them. Elliot heard something hit the floor, and he pushed himself forward so he could look through the doorframe to the next room. Soldiers were rushing to the windows, returning fire from there. Elliot saw what had landed on the floor, seemingly unrecognized by anyone else—a round, white metal grenade. He dived behind the wall with his hands over his ears, just as the grenade exploded. A part of the wall was blasted away. Screams could be heard everywhere now. There came another explosion, further down the corridor. A body slammed against the corridor wall then collapsed, joining the piles of dead. The door crashed opened, and Elliot saw Boyd get to his feet, drawing his handgun. Before he could shoot even once, a bullet hit his shoulder. Miller had taken cover in the room next to him and dashed into the corridor, his assault rifle blazing at the intruders. The two Russians were caught in the bullet storm and danced like puppets on electric strings as the projectiles ripped into them. Elliot went to all fours and grabbed Boyd, pushing him out of the corridor into the next room. Then he kicked at the door to close it.

"Take it!" Boyd panted and held out his handgun to Elliot. Not really a fan of guns, Elliot took it and checked it was armed and had a bullet in the chamber. He had learned a few things about these. The only thing he hadn't learned, was getting comfortable with them. Looking at the door outside, he heard automatic weapons being fired. After the successful ambush, the American soldiers had let their guards down; there now followed a very angry exchange of shots.

A clonking sound behind him made Elliot turn. A hook had come through the window. His heart, beat like crazy, then seemed to stop for a moment. His breathing went flat, and instead an unhealthy dose of adrenaline surged through him. With a trembling hand, he raised the handgun and put his second hand under it for support. Aiming like he was on a shooting range, he saw the hook move from side to side as someone climbed up. Elliot glanced at Boyd, who had noticed this too.

Elliot waited; every second seemed to stretch into an eternity. There was a clicking sound, and a second later, another of the white hand grenades flew into the room, clonking to a crest only three-feet away from him. Seconds. That's all he had. Elliot leaped forward, grabbed it, and threw it right back out the window. It was only just through the frame when it exploded. Elliot was pushed back by the shockwave and felt a searing pain in his leg, as his back rammed into the wall. Gasping in agony, he looked down and saw a piece of metal had burned through his snowsuit and was stuck in his leg. It was only superficial, but the pain was actually radiating through his whole limb. Giving himself a moment to breathe, he looked for Boyd, who was still on the floor covering his head.

"Are you alright?" he asked Elliot, holding his shoulder.

"My leg caught a shrapnel, I think. But nothing too bad," Elliot hissed as he pushed himself up. The leg was still functional, supporting his weight, but it hurt to move. Unfortunately, he had to. Raising the gun again, this time with one hand, he made his way to the window—what remained of it. There was a large hole now where the window had been. The wind was bitingly cold as it entered through it. Shielding his face from the snow that blew

171

vertically right at him, Elliot stepped forward and lowered the gun. The Russian wasn't dead; he was almost not recognizable as a human anymore; the explosion having torn him completely apart. Elliot felt surprised that he didn't even feel the need to vomit. Either he had got harder over time, or it was the mix of shock and adrenaline.

"Base secured!" Miller shouted from outside.

"Let's hope this time he means it," Boyd said; pushing himself up against the wall.

"We need a medic for you," Elliot said, and Boyd nodded.

"Guess some guys outside there need one more urgently. Bullet went straight through, and as I'm still alive, I guess it hit no artery or anything." Boyd clenched his teeth. "Damn painful though."

Miller entered the room now, showing relief to see them both alive. "We lost eight of our men," he reported.

"Dammit!" Boyd gasped.

"Another two injured. Leaving us with . . ." Miller swallowed.

"Eight?" Boyd guessed.

"Seven, sir," he answered. "With most of them in Base One now. We should evacuate it just in case we have one more stroller out there," Miller said.

"Okay, get a medic to have a quick look at his leg, then we'll go. We'll take the tunnel," Boyd said, and Miller helped him up.

"Wait, what tunnel?" Elliot asked. Boyd just laughed.

Chapter 16

Ashra watched as another explosion ripped through Base Two. Whatever happened there, the fight was seemingly not over, and from here, the snowdrifts now covering the plains blocked her sight.

"You think we're winning?" Gustavsson asked and stood next to her.

"Hard to say. But I don't think either side will be left without casualties," Ashra said, then turned to Gustavsson. The man sighed and pushed his glasses up on his nose. Ashra turned back to the fighting. From afar, she heard the shooting.

"You and Elliot are now all that's left of our science division," she said. "I hope you're up for the task."

"I'm hardly a scientist. I predict weather, which, yes is a bit of physics, but I don't even have a doctorate," he said. "Also, I can't believe Jordan did that. I mean, it's so terrible."

"Well, I guess we really don't know him. I imagine a sleeper agent plays a role; he just plays it for so long it becomes almost indistinguishable from himself." Ashra shrugged. Gustavsson turned back to his computer.

"The storm will pass quickly. Approximately an hour. It lost a lot of its force when it turned," he reported, as if Ashra had asked. Ashra didn't really care about the storm, as long as she knew Elliot was OK. She left and turned down the corridor. Passing McKenzie and her men, all looking out of the windows with worried expressions, she finally made it to Boyd's bureau. As she opened the door, she saw Jordan rage against the restraints, mumbling something impossible to understand into the gag in his mouth. Ashra closed the door without her eyes leaving him. The youngest of the three scientists Boyd had drafted into service, had lost his glasses in the attempt to free himself. They lay in front of him on the floor. Ashra went over and picked them up, then gave him a gentle smile.

"If you stay calm, I'll put them back on your head," Ashra said, and he immediately stopped raging against the stainless- steel cuffs. Was he trying to break loose? Steel handcuffs were impossible to break with human strength. You couldn't even bend them the slightest bit if you didn't have the strength of ten men. "Boyd wants me to kill you," Ashra said. Jordan shook his head with tears in his eyes.

"Problem is, I have a question, one only you can answer. Ready?"

Jordan nodded.

"Why the timer?" Ashra asked. "You could have used some Wi-Fi connector, maybe a raspberry pie even, to set the bomb off whenever you needed to. Right? A Bluetooth plug-in? Of course, we both know why. You followed your training. Acquired the explosive and used a timer just as you had been trained. Trained in the late nineties, early twenty-first century probably, before we had Wi-Fi connections and Bluetooth. Yet, here's the problem. You're too young to be trained back then. Way too young." Ashra shook her head. "I guess you aren't our man after all."

"Smart. I had the feeling you suspected me." The voice came from behind. Gustavsson stood there, pointing a small handgun with a silencer directly at her. "Scream and you both die," he said.

"We'll die anyway." Ashra got up. "Right before you."

"Yeah, maybe, but it's for a greater good, if that gives you comfort." Gustavsson said. "Damn Gernsbeck surprised me. Everything was going so nicely until then. Nobody suspects the fat guy, right? The comic relief?" Gustavsson stepped forward.

"Since when?"

"From the start. Sleeper agent—figured that one out right. Makes sense, weather and all that. Everyone asks us for the weather, even the military." Gustavsson slowly circled her. "Set him free."

"So you can make it look as if he was it?" Ashra snorted. "Listen, it's over. Your guys are all dead. There's no play you can win here." Ashra took one step toward the overweight man, and he raised his gun to aim at her head.

"Of course, I'm the villain and you're the hero, right, Professor? I'm Russian. Hollywood told us the Russians are always the bad guys, so obviously I have to be." He rolled his eyes.

"Just out of pure interest, you feel killing a bunch of people might have had any influence on your image? Just asking because it obviously did." Ashra shrugged, and he laughed.

"War causes casualties. I was sorry about it. Especially Gernsbeck. He just walked in on me. Had to improvise." His fingers loosened their grip, then tightened again.

"So what now? You'll kill us all? Is it that?" Ashra asked.

"Something like that," Gustavsson said. "What gave me away?"

"The sweater. You changed clothes. Who does that when under siege? You had to, of course. Blood on it, I guess," Ashra said. "Then Jordan just didn't fit. All we had on him came from you."

175

"And here I was, thinking nobody suspects the fat guy. Get on your knees, hands behind your head!" he ordered.

"If you shoot me, the soldiers will be here within ten seconds."

"Yeah, I know. Take out your gun with two fingers, slowly," Gustavsson looked at Jordan still tied to the pipe, and glaring at him. Ashra's hand slid behind her back, and Gustavsson's eyes were on her again.

"*Slowly*," he said, still aiming at her head. She wondered if she could dodge the bullet, draw, and shoot before he unloaded the entire magazine at this short distance. Probably not. She slowly took the gun from her belt and held it to the side.

"Drop it," Gustavsson said, and Ashra let it go, her eyes not leaving him. Gustavsson's eyes didn't leave her either. Then from his belt he drew a blade. Long, thin, but sharp looking, it rotated in his palm—so he didn't plan to shoot her.

She knew she should scream, but if she did, he would pull the trigger. The best chance to stop him and escape alive, was for him to actually come closer to slit her throat.

Which was exactly what he did.

With one emotionless move, he raised the knife and approached her, bringing the knife to her throat, intending to cut it before she even realized what was going on.

Ashra let the blade come close. The world slowed down around her; as adrenaline and her training kicked in, sharpening her senses. Her hand came up and easily deflected his, redirecting the force of his attack to make the blade miss. Then everything happened so fast. Her hand grabbed the gun, and the one she had used to block snapped forward, hitting his throat. Gustavsson made one gurgling sound, but he was no longer the nerdy overweight man—he moved with the grace of a trained killer. Pushing his knee up, he hit her chest, and the air was forced out of her lungs. The blade came around again, and she just brought her arm up fast enough—to take the cut meant for her throat. Gasping in pain, she threw herself backwards, hoping he would let go of his gun. He didn't. Instead, he followed her movement, the knife now up in the air to stab down. Ashra let go of the gun and rolled aside. The blade rammed into the floor. Gustavsson didn't waste any time pulling it out he raised the gun to shoot her. At this range he could unload the magazine into her without any problems. Ashra had her own gun now though, and as she rolled, she brought it up and fired a single shot.

Gustavsson's movement ended mid-air and his eyes opened, possibly going blind as the bullet entered his skull between his eyes and shattered his glasses. The upper cut this was called—the spot where the brain's stem met the spine. If shot there, the lights just went out. Which was what Ashra saw in his eyes as he collapsed—the light going out. She lowered her gun and looked at Jordan.

He barked into his gag.

"Guess you're telling me you told me so?" she asked. "Or do you want me to untie you?" Ashra reached into her pocket to get the keys out. "Because you're probably right about both."

The door burst open, and McKenzie came in, rifle first.

"We're good! He's dead," she said.

"Gustavsson?" McKenzie looked at him, still holding his pistol and the knife stuck in the ground.

"Yeah, I got our traitor." Ashra forced herself up. "Let's hope the others took care of his friends."

"They did. But heavy losses. Brand is injured, so is Boyd," McKenzie said.

Ashra threw her the keys and stormed out.

****

Elliot was walking with a limp, his leg now having a tight emergency bandage around it, applied by the field medic. He smiled as he saw Ashra waiting for him at the ledge; she offered him a hand to help him up.

"Damn tough guy for a professor," Boyd said, his arm now resting in a sling.

"Yeah, I know." Ashra smiled as Elliot arrived at the base. "Gustavsson was the traitor."

Elliot looked up. "Really? He was my least likely suspect."

"Yeah, that's what he was good at. Really just an accident I found out. He tried to kill me."

"But assuming we're still talking to you, I assume it didn't go as planned?" Boyd said.

"He's dead. Even kept my promise and used your gun," Ashra answered.

"Nice. In five in the lab." He made his way to his office, now the scene of the infiltrators' demise.

Elliot watched him go, and Ashra used the moment to give him a hug, as the other soldiers climbed out of the hatch.

"They killed them, all of them," Elliot said. "It was a slaughter."

"I can imagine. You were there?" Ashra asked.

"Right in the middle of it," Elliot said as she stepped back; his jacket was covered in drying blood. He took it off and threw it aside before limping toward the lab. "We need to get to work. We don't have much time."

Ashra followed him, smiling to herself. To hell with the Russians, at least she had Elliot back. Although, she already saw in his face she wouldn't like what he had to say.

They gathered in the lab where Jordan was sitting at his laptop. He glanced up as they entered, giving Ashra an angry look.

"You okay?" Elliot asked him.

"Yeah." He nodded. "Despite the circumstances, I'd say I'm all right."

McKenzie entered next, then Miller. Finally, Boyd came into the room and closed the door. Jordan threw him the same look.

"I won't apologize if you're waiting for that. My call. I made the best I could," Boyd said.

"What about the prisoners?" Elliot asked. Ashra raised her eyebrows. So they had prisoners.

"Locked in the mess, hands restrained, two of my men guarding them," Miller replied. Elliot nodded.

"So please, tell us what you found." He addressed Elliot who sat down in a chair. Ashra sat on the table next to him.

"It's not good," Elliot said. Then he began telling his tale from the ancient ruins and about the ancestor race that had once lived there.

****

When he was finally done, a silence lingered between them. It took almost a minute until Boyd spoke.

"How fast is this thing charging?" he asked.

"I wanted to ask Gernsbeck, since he's the physics guy. But I think it grows exponentially, which means we appear to have a problem," Elliot said.

"Yeah, thanks for that." Boyd sighed and looked at McKenzie. Ashra didn't like that look. She knew exactly what it referred to.

"The energy is contained, but that containment will fail sooner or later. If not, the pillar itself seemed to be getting to its limits. It might be a matter of days or hours. So we need to act quickly. Whatever machine was used by the Ancestors that needed that much energy is no longer there, and that makes this reactor—I assume—practically a bomb," Elliot concluded.

"I think you got it all wrong, Professor."

Everybody turned now to the voice that had so far been silent on the matter. McKenzie gave them a thin smile. "With all due respect."

"Soldier, leave the science to the experts." Ashra turned her back on McKenzie.

"No. I'd like to hear what you have to say. What did I get wrong?" Elliot said.

"Well, this was a major facility to this Ancestors, right? Probably their only facility with this giant energy source. What would we do to secure such a resource?"

"We would hide it, guard it, and if possible, try to keep it a secret," Boyd said and looked to McKenzie. She shrugged.

"Before I became spec-ops, I served on a nuclear submarine. Alabama Class. Stuffed with nuclear warheads. Hidden, armed to the teeth, top secret locations and all that. But in case all failed, we had one more fail safe to make sure our nukes would never get into the wrong hands," McKenzie said.

"Self-destruction." Ashra realized what she meant.

"Guess how we would do it?" McKenzie asked.

"Overloading the reactor?" Ashra was again the one guessing.

"Exactly." McKenzie nodded.

"So they blow up a bomb in Antarctica, that's it?" Boyd asked.

"Back then Antarctica was probably a population center. What do we know?" Elliot said. "But I think that isn't what this is about. The explosion combined with the electromagnetic pulse it releases are the problem. I've been thinking about it. What could this thing do? I think when it goes up the explosion might cause the magnetic field of earth to fail. That's why it was built on the pole and that's why it needs so much energy."

"What does that mean? It destroys our electromagnetic field? Compasses won't work?"

"It means the atmosphere of planet Earth might fail and dissolve. Air could slowly diffuse into space, and unprotected against solar storms, the surface of our planet would soon be scorched earth. Look at Mars and you get an idea what planets without an atmosphere look like." Elliot glanced at Ashra.

"Okay, that means—" Ashra began.

"It was a trap. From the beginning, the Ancestors meant for their reactor to become a trap if they weren't around to keep it from happening."

"These guys wanted to destroy all life on Earth if they died out?" Boyd asked.

"I think they wanted their enemy to die in case they lost the war and were exterminated, yes. The relief seemed to show a battle, and these gray ants obviously were some sort of weapon system. I think the Ancestors were warriors," Elliot said.

"Wouldn't we do the same?" Ashra asked. "Would humanity accept extinction? I guess we would launch every weapon in our nuclear arsenal and end the world, too."

Elliot nodded. He had never been into politics. But from what he knew about humans, that scenario seemed not unlikely. "And would we spend a single thought on the future civilizations made of super-smart dolphins or cockroaches? The thought what we took from them wouldn't even pass our mind," Elliot added. "To the Ancestors, we're nothing. An obscure second chance at intelligent life was probably nothing they even took into consideration."

"So, what will we do?" Boyd asked.

"We need to stop the reaction," Elliot said. "By any means possible."

Boyd looked at him, and Ashra could see the thought behind his eyes.

"Boyd, you can't be thinking of what I think you're thinking!" Ashra said.

"Thanks for your excellent work. We'll take it from here," Boyd said.

"Boyd!" Ashra said, as he walked toward the door.

"What is it?" Elliot asked. Ashra realized she never had a chance to tell him.

"He has a tactical nuclear warhead here. They're hiding it in the depot," Ashra said. Elliot stared at Boyd, and Ashra felt he might attack him.

"You have *what*?" Elliot asked incredulously.

"This information is classified," Boyd replied.

"Listen, that's . . . the most stupid plan we could possibly come up with. What is it you want to do with it? Blow the entire place up?" Elliot said.

"That's exactly what I'll do. Destroy the facility and all that's in it. Eradicate the danger this reactor poses to all of us."

"Boyd, this is an energy core contained by means we can't even comprehend. If you set off a nuke right next to it, you might trigger it to overload and explode," Elliot raised his hands in a defensive gesture. "I have a better plan."

"And how sure are you yours will work?" Boyd asked.

"Fifty, fifty," Elliot admitted.

"Well, I'm fully confident in mine. Nukes don't set things off. They vaporize everything in their proximity, basically turning it to gas," Boyd said.

"Energy can't become gas," Jordan said. Boyd turned to him. "The professor is right. It'll discharge at best, but more likely it'll blow up."

Boyd stared at him. "You're not a physicist and neither is Professor Brand."

"Neither are you, moron," Jordan stared at Boyd. The CIA man tilted his head.

"What did you just call me?" he asked.

Jordan stood up now. "Idiot. That's clearly what you are. Beyond average intelligence they call it, right? Retard? Been told that's no longer politically correct, but anyway, it seems fitting. Shithead?"

"Guys, we should probably discuss this properly," Elliot said, but Ashra saw it was too late for that. Boyd turned to Elliot.

"I think you made clear we have no time," he said. "So the idiot calls the shots here, and I say we turn this damn place into a glass desert." With these words, he took out his gun in one fluent draw and held it to Jordan's head. Before Ashra could draw hers, he pulled the trigger.

Jordan's eyes were still widened in shock as he fell back. Ashra's gun was immediately in her hands, but as she brought it up, she saw Miller and McKenzie both aiming at her head. Ashra aimed at Boyd's head and clenched her teeth.

"What now? You want to kill me?" Boyd asked.

"Why did you do that?" Elliot yelled.

"Because I can and because I don't need him anymore," Boyd said. "I hope you aren't losing your usefulness too soon,

Professor," Boyd hissed. Then he turned to Ashra again. Ashra was still aiming her gun right between his eyes. Thoughts raced through her mind. If she shot him, she would die a second later. An acceptable price if it meant saving life on planet Earth. Boyd seemed to read her mind and sneered at her.

"No? Not shooting?" he asked. "Miller, if she pulls that trigger, I want you to kill Professor Brand in front of her eyes. Then execute the plan without me. McKenzie has everything she needs for it," Boyd said, still staring at Ashra.

"You're insane," Elliot hissed, but then slowly reached for Ashra's gun and pressed it down. Miller grabbed the gun and pushed her to her knees, putting his pistol to her head.

"No. We might need her to motivate the professor here who seems so fond of her. I guess he won't work for us out of patriotism anymore." Boyd sighed. "Bring them to the Russians, then we should prepare," Boyd said, and McKenzie stepped forward, taking Elliot.

"What if you're wrong? Would you risk the entire planet just because you think you're afraid?" Elliot asked.

"I won't risk it because I'm afraid. Professor, I'll do what I have to," Boyd said. Ashra was already being dragged out and pushed to the door. Miller's grip was strong, and she knew she had little hope to overcome him. A trained and experienced fighter like him would have subdued stronger opponents than her. She considered trying anyway. It was Elliot's look that kept her from doing so. He was right, of course. To stop him, they had to stop the entire thing, not put a bullet in Boyd's head. She would enjoy doing that.

Chapter 17

"He's clearly lost his mind." Elliot tried one last time to make the two soldiers see reason.

"Shut up," McKenzie replied.

"You follow the orders of a madman. He just killed Jordan for Christ's sake. Does that mean nothing to you?" he asked.

"We never wanted to leave witnesses," McKenzie said. Ashra's expression told him that she already knew that.

"You mean you brought us here to kill us eventually? And you guys consider yourselves the good guys?" Elliot asked.

"We consider ourselves nothing but soldiers," Miller answered. "We have our orders, and we'll follow them."

Pierce stood next to the door of the mess and opened it quickly as his superior approached.

He had one last attempt before they would be shoved into the mess. "Miller, this isn't about being a good man or a soldier. This isn't about following orders. If you blow up the reactor, it will blow up! Logic says it will! What would happen if you threw a nuke on a nuclear reactor, hmm? It would blow up! This thing is bigger than all nuclear reactors combined. This is about the end of the world!" Elliot implored.

"Have a little faith, Professor," Miller said and shoved him into the mess. Ashra landed right next to him, and the door was closed.

"If they attempt to escape, kill them," Miller ordered the guards outside.

Elliot went to the door and kicked it in a rage, forgetting his leg was injured. The pain almost knocked him out, and he sank down against the wall. There were five Russians staring at them. They had managed to get rid of their restraints and rubbed their wrists. The colonel smiled at Brand as he saw him sitting there.

"Trouble in paradise, Professor?" he asked.

"Well, the end of paradise, I'd say. Our American friend is about to blow up the damn planet," Elliot said.

"How does he plan on doing that?" The colonel stepped forward.

"By detonating a nuclear warhead right next to a reactor a hundred times more powerful than anything we've built," Elliot said.

"He has a nuclear warhead, a portable one," Ashra explained.

"I see." The colonel sighed. "Not that it makes a big difference now."

"Oh, the end of the world doesn't make a difference? This thing will blow our atmosphere away like you blow out a match." Elliot forced himself up.

"Well, may I share a little information with you? Classified of course, but who gives a damn about classifications, hmm?" the colonel stepped forward.

"What have you done?" Elliot asked.

"Nothing. That's the problem. If I stay silent for more than an hour, two Tupolev Tu-160 long distance bombers will be on their way with the orders to eradicate this site," he said.

"You stupid . . ."

"Oh, we didn't know about the danger," the colonel said. "It made strategic sense to have a backup plan."

"Did Gustavsson not tell you?" Ashra snapped at him, and the man looked up at her.

"Oh, you found him?" he said.

"What will those bombers do?"

"They use hypersonic missiles. They'll target the ruins and fire two of those rather expensive warheads. The strongest non-conventional weapon in our arsenal," the colonel said.

"When?" Elliot asked.

"Exactly in two hours and thirty minutes," the colonel answered.

"You military idiots. Can none of you accept that this is a power beyond your comprehension developed by a civilization that rose and fell long before ours was even in its early stages? Is it too much to ask for any of you to think before you apply your primitive standard tactics of blowing everything up that you feel threatened by?" Elliot felt so furious he wanted to punch him.

"I'm afraid if you ask a hammer to solve a problem, Professor, all the problems in the world would need to be nails," he said. Elliot stared at him. He almost had to respect the amount of self-reflection the man showed.

"Ashra, we need to get out of here," Elliot said.

"The windows have been sealed," Ashra replied. "Maybe we can rip out some of the ground plates."

"We already tried that. Would take hours to loosen the screws without proper equipment," the colonel replied.

"Listen." Elliot took a deep breath. He knew he needed allies. More than anything, right now he needed allies to get out of here and stop the CIA madman who was in charge of this operation. "If I find a way for us to get out of here, will you help us? Will you recall your bombers and help us stop Boyd Green?"

"The bombers are too high to be reached and have been ordered to keep strict radio silence. Bombing a target in Antarctica isn't exactly legal," the colonel said.

"You said we can switch the machine off?" Ashra asked. "You said you have an idea?"

"The crystals. I believe they run some sort of infinite operational system that kept the reactor going all those years and powered it up once oxygen was available. It's just an idea, but I think that they took the effort, incredible effort to build that computer, that they're essential for the reactor. If we destroy them, we can probably . . . the reactor might shut down. At least it might not charge anymore," Elliot said.

Ashra stared at him. She was smart enough to know there was a difference now. If the reactor shut down, it would mean they were safe. If the Russians blew up the place anyway and that energy source was still in it? It would mean the thing would go up.

"That's the best you got?" Ashra asked.

"I'm afraid so," he answered.

"Then we need to shut it down before the Russians bomb the place. Or in other words, within two hours and thirty minutes." Ashra looked at the colonel. "So are you in or not?"

The colonel sighed. "I'll be court martialed for this, but at least there will be someone left to bring me before a court. We'll help you. But how will you get us out of here?"

"I bet on the most unreliable source of strength in the entire world," Elliot said. "A reasonable mind." With those words, he turned to the door and limped over. Ashra followed him, ready to catch him if he fell over.

"Pierce," Elliot said. "I know you're out there. I know you've seen what I've seen. That giant ball of light, that energy. Like a second sun. That alien place, buried in the ice down there. I know you've seen it too! Listen to me. If Boyd Green blows that place up, if he activates the bomb in there, that ball of energy will blow up. Do you know what happens if the sun blows up?" Elliot leaned his head against the door. "I know I'm not a soldier. I can't give any orders, and God knows I'm bad at following them. Right now though, there are two groups in this building. It's not Russians and Americans. The two groups are those men who are too scared, too blind, too angry to see what they're doing. Those men will be the end of all life on this planet if they succeed. Every bug, every plant, every human being will perish. There will never be life on this Earth again. The other group will do anything to not let that happen. All those who belong to this group, the one trying to save us all, are all locked inside here," Elliot said. "Or aren't they?" Elliot put his hands against the wall. Somehow, he knew the young soldier was listening. "I'm asking you to disobey a direct order from your superiors. I'm asking you to let us out of here. If you do that, I promise I'll do everything within my power to stop this madness. If you don't do it, you'll die a good soldier. And everything else, everything . . . will die with you." There was again

191

only silence. "I understand if you don't believe me. I mean, we barely know each other. But I had a mentor once, a man I loved and yet . . . we had our differences. I didn't believe him either. I'll regret it for the rest of my life because he was right, and I was wrong." Elliot sighed. "Good thing is you won't have much time to regret it, I assume." Silence again. Then he heard a man outside yelp.

"What are you doing?" a young voice asked.

"Holding a gun to your head so you can later say I forced you to open the door," Pierce replied. "Open it."

The lock was opened, and Pierce, holding his pistol only loosely toward the direction of his comrade, opened the door. Elliot smiled at him.

"Thanks."

"Don't thank me. Tell me what we can do," he said.

"The nuclear device is in the depot. We need to get there and make sure they don't bring it to the ruins," Ashra said.

"We're going to need weapons!" the colonel said. Pierce nodded and looked at his colleague.

"You won't need that. I'll help you," the young man said to Pierce. Elliot saw the name label said Roberts.

"Equipment room at the end of the corridor." Pierce took his assault rifle from his shoulder, handing Elliot the handgun, which Elliot gave to Ashra. Roberts drew his pistol and handed this to him too. "Okay," Elliot said as Ashra loaded her gun and went to the lab.

"Where are the others?" she asked.

"Miller took them with him," Pierce said. Outside, the storm was now raging with all its might. Ashra stared out through the large window in the lab.

"Good news is they'll have a hard time getting it there with this weather," Ashra said.

"Bad news is, so will we," Elliot said. The colonel now showed up, armed with an American assault rifle, several hand grenades, and a handgun. He had a sniper rifle and handed it to Elliot; who looked surprised.

"How good a shot are you?" he asked.

"I'm a terrible shot," Elliot replied.

"Well, with your leg, you can go nowhere, so you'll give us cover. Just shoot in the general direction of our enemies so they keep their head down," the colonel instructed.

"I'll come with you," Elliot insisted, not planning to leave this to others. It felt unfair. In a way, he felt responsible, simply because he had delivered the bad news.

"You'd slow us down," Ashra said. "You can join us when . . . it's over," she said, as another Russian appeared and handed her an assault rifle with a scope. She bowed her head gratefully, then turned to the colonel.

"Your mission, your lead," Ashra said. The colonel got his rifle ready in both hands. Pulling his ski mask on, his men all armed their weapons and followed him as he passed their lines. Pierce and Roberts took the rear, and Ashra stepped into the middle of the men. Elliot watched them as they made their way to the door. They just needed to open the lock, and it hammered open as the wind made its way inside. He saw them leave and looked down at the rifle. Not that he would see much out there. But he had to do what he could. He looked for an optimal position, from where he could at least see what was happening out there.

Chapter 18

The colonel went first, and like all of them, he had to lean against the wind to even move forward. With heavy steps, he made his way into the wall of white, the snowdrifts whipping against him. Ashra felt the cold against her face even through the ski mask. The storm was merciless, but it would also hide their approach. What would have otherwise been a walk of over six-hundred-feet of unprotected snow plains, was now an invisible approach in the endless whiteout.

The colonel pointed. He was still oriented even in this environment. Ashra herself found this difficult, and snowstorms had been a big part of her youth. None like this though. The ferocity of the icy wind was frightening. She felt like if she lost her tension, she would simply be blown away. Checking her watch, she saw they had two hours and fifteen minutes left. Looking around, she realized someone could be standing six-feet from her and she wouldn't see them. The whiteout deserved its name. Embedded in the Russian soldiers, she kept on pushing forward at the same speed as them. These were tough men, forcing their way through the wind, unimpressed by the elements of nature.

Then suddenly the wind grew much less intense. As if they had reached the eye of a tornado, the snow began to float around them and slowly set to the ground. The sun broke through and made the snowflakes shimmer. A strange beauty rested in this moment. Then a hiss beside her ripped her out of her dreamlike moment and instinctively she dropped to the ground, brought her weapon up, and started to fire in the general direction of the enemy. The depot lay there, coated in orange metal plates. She saw a muzzle flare from under it. A Russian to her side collapsed.

Ashra took aim and fired three rounds at the position where the muzzle flare had come from; then another three and another three. By the third burst, all of the Russians were returning fire on the attackers. Boyd's remaining men. They had waited for them. The dead body of a soldier collapsed on her legs, and she had to clench her teeth to fight down the pain.

"Contact!" the colonel yelled, and she saw him leaving the relative safety of a pile of snow. Firing, he charged toward the enemy line and fired burst after burst. Ashra couldn't stand up with the soldier on her legs, so instead aimed and fired in the same direction, giving the colonel cover as good as she could. After a few more bursts the gun announced it was empty with a loud click. She reached down to her replacement magazine but found it hard to reach. Trying to pull herself out from under the dead soldier, her hands slipped in the snowy ground. As she looked up, she saw the colonel collapse in the snow, the red of his blood spraying from a dozen wounds as he was hit again and again.

Then there was silence. Deadly, absolute silence. Ashra let go of her rifle and grabbed her handgun. She couldn't load it with her gloves on, so she bit into her fingers and dragged the glove off her hand. Loading the weapon, she turned forward as a single soldier with a pistol approached them. A Russian tried to crawl away, but the man pointed the gun at his head and pulled the trigger. The Russian collapsed. Ashra tried to take aim. She pulled the trigger. She *tried* to pull it. Frozen. The handgun had frozen in the icy wind. Tossing it down on the ground she tried again, but it didn't work. The man smiled as he removed the ski mask. A soldier, her age.

"Looks like you ran out of luck, traitor," he said with a southern U.S. accent, as he raised the gun. Ashra closed her eyes. So this was how it would happen. She would fail Elliot, the entire planet, and die, shot by a man she'd considered an ally, who didn't understand the wrongfulness of his orders. A bullet that would doom the entire world. A bullet taking away humanity's final chance of being saved from a trap so ancient, one could hardly acknowledge it. She heard the shot. Opening her eyes, the man, who was unharmed, raised his gun and fired at Base One. A futile attempt at this distance, no matter how good a shot he was. Why was Elliot such a bad shot? A second shot hit the snow next to the man, and he grimaced, then turned to Ashra. He held the gun straight at her head, and Ashra tried to grab it. The moment she reached it, the hand of the man was no longer there. Five shots rang over the icefield, all hitting him in the chest. He crumpled next to her. Ashra gasped out and looked over her shoulder. Leaning against a pile of snow, holding his side was Pierce— lowering his handgun he had just killed his comrade with.

Ashra began thrashing and finally broke free of the man on top of her. Crawling over to Peirce, she took the dead soldier's gun. At least this one seemed to work just fine. She knelt next to Pierce. He was terribly pale, and blood was flowing from the wound at his side. Ashra pressed on it, but she saw it made little sense.

"That was Matthew. He was my friend," Pierce said with a weak voice.

"I'm sorry. We need to . . ."

"No. You need to complete the mission," Pierce said. "I won't be around to see the end of it anyway."

Ashra closed her eyes and knew he was right; she had no time to attend to his wound, and it would only prolong his suffering. The young man was about to die. Tears in her eyes, she let go of his wound and crawled back.

"Can I do anything for you?" Ashra asked.

197

"Just end the mission," he gasped. Ashra nodded and stood up. She grabbed one of the assault rifles off a dead soldier—and one of the hand grenades.

"Ashra." She heard the voice behind her; Elliot was holding the sniper rifle and limping toward her. Without the storm, he was much faster.

"We need to keep them from—" Ashra hissed and signaled him to lower himself, to not present such an excellent target.

"Too late." Elliot pointed to Base Two, and Ashra needed a moment to understand what she was meant to see. A snowcat was missing. There was only one left.

"Damn. They're delivering the package." She got up. Stomping toward the Russian vehicles, Elliot limped after her.

"Ashra!" he called. "What are you doing?"

"Those things look a little clumsy, but I bet they're way more powerful than a snowcat. I'll make a few minutes on them," she said.

"Ashra," Elliot called again, no longer able to keep up. "Ashra!"

"We have no time, Elliot!"

"We need the backpack I had. The corridor with the gray ants, you need that crystal as a light source," Elliot gasped.

"Where is it?" Ashra asked.

Elliot looked around and shook his head. "I don't know.".

Ashra checked her watch. Under two hours now. She began to run to the dead American soldier. From the corner of her eye, she had seen something at his belt. She turned him around and found what she was looking for. Two tin-like grenades. One explosive. She grabbed all three and pushed them into her jacket.

"What's that?" Elliot asked.

"Flashbangs. Sends a bright light through a phosphor core explosion," she said.

"They used them when they attacked."

"Okay, I have to go," she wanted to run, but Elliot tugged her arm.

"I'll go." He looked into her eyes.

"Your leg slows you down," she said.

"We have an hour and forty minutes. I needed ninety minutes to get there. I was very careful though, so I can make it in an hour and ten probably," he said.

"With your leg, you can't do it at all," Ashra replied.

"It's okay, I can inject myself with morphine on the way."

"Elliot . . ." She shook her head.

"Listen, I know the path, you don't," Elliot said.

"I memorized it when you went. I'll find it," Ashra said.

"Ashra, I need twenty minutes there. That means whoever goes up there, if they make it up there in an hour and ten minutes, they barely have ten minutes to escape the ruins." His grip on her arm became stronger.

"Whoever goes . . . Also needs to kill two soldiers and disarm the nuclear bomb they carry. Which means that whoever goes there will have no time at all to get out of there." Ashra looked at him. "Whoever goes there . . . doesn't need that time though."

"No, I'll go," Elliot said, "Ashra . . ."

"You have a mission here. Boyd. He has a remote control for the bomb. It makes no sense to deactivate it if he can detonate it from afar," she said. "They won't have taken them with them. He's injured. A liability." Ashra jerked her head to the depot. "He'll still be here."

"Ashra. You take care of Boyd. I can . . ."

"No." Ashra stepped closer to him; her hand, now freezing cold, touched his face. "You can't. Elliot. This time you can't go. You can't save me or the planet. It has to be me," Ashra said, and tears rushed to her eyes. It had to be her. She realized that long ago. Not only because she was the logical choice, but because Elliot was too valuable to the world. He was too smart, too dedicated to die. Most of all though . . .

"I love you," Ashra said. She leaned forward to kiss him. Elliot trembled under her kiss. She wished she could just stand there and kiss him until the world ended. But she knew she couldn't. She felt him move to embrace her, but she pushed him away. With his injured leg, he lost his balance and fell into the snow. "Get Boyd!" she said and ran toward the nearest Russian tracked armored transport.

Elliot remained in the snow, watching her leave.

Chapter 19

Elliot saw her climb into the tank-like vehicle, and it began moving almost immediately. She was either familiar with it, or her desperation was enough to make her understand it.

"I love you, too," Elliot said; more to himself than to Ashra, who could no longer hear him. Too late. As always, he said everything too late to Ashra Shah. He would never see her again. Trembling, he turned around and forced himself to his feet. Actually, he *knew* who was responsible for him losing her, and he would die or honor her last wish.

Limping forward, he threw away the rifle that he had no idea how to use, and took out the handgun Roberts had given him. He passed Roberts lying dead in the snow. Pierce was there too. The Russians. The colonel had got a little closer to the depot before being killed.

Loading the gun, Elliot saw the door was open. Someone had seemingly destroyed the lock mechanism. His bet would be on Ashra. Even thinking her name made him upset. Wiping the tears from his eyes, he entered the depot as silently as possible. Inside, he listened and heard steps. Looking around, he saw a staircase between the crates and light coming from it. Boyd wasn't hiding. Good.

Kneeling down sent a wave of agony through him, but he gritted his teeth and ignored it, loosened his boots, and gently slipped out of them. The floor was warm. He crept forward, making no sound as his soft socks padded on the ground. The gun raised, aimed in the direction he was walking toward, he stepped on the metal steps. The metal grid cut into his soles, but he inched his way down. Boyd's legs were the first thing he saw. Then he saw him whole, standing at a table, leaning over it. On the table was a large metal box with a rather long antenna and a single red button. Next to it, lay the pistol he had given to Ashra earlier. His personal weapon.

"Don't move." Elliot aimed at Boyd's torso. He wouldn't risk missing the head. No, if he tried to reach for the weapon, he would simply empty his magazine into the man's body. Pale, his face covered with sweat and a strand of hair glued to his forehead, Boyd closed his eyes, then gave a short laugh.

"Professor, what does a man need to do for you to deserve to die?"

"Blowing up the atmosphere of our planet might do the trick, but we're working on it," Elliot said.

"They have a ten-minute head start. The moment the shooting began, they took off," Boyd said.

"Ashra isn't that easy to shake off, believe me." Elliot arrived at the end of the stairs. "Step away from the table."

"I don't know. I have the feeling you've never killed someone before. It's not as easy as you think." Boyd's hand moved. Elliot raised his gun. Boyd froze.

"Regrettably for both of us, that's not true," Elliot answered, still aiming at him.

"That Russian doesn't count. That was pure instinctive self-defense." Boyd scowled. "I mean *kill* someone. End his life."

"The Russian wasn't my first. I hope for both of us he'll be my last," Elliot said, now standing opposite Boyd, aiming right at him. Boyd looked at him for a moment.

"Oh, I see," he said. "We need to destroy these ruins. You and your scientific curiosity might find that intolerable, but it's the truth," he almost hissed the words.

"They will be destroyed. You and the Russians actually wanted the same all along. Kill each other, destroy the ruins. You would have been great friends. You know?"

"One doesn't make friends with his enemies."

"Yeah, I get that now. Just hard to see who the enemy is sometimes." Elliot straightened his back. "Step back. Final warning."

Boyd raised his free hand and took a step back from the table. "You sent her to her death then?" he asked.

"I didn't *send* her anywhere. Ashra isn't the one who takes orders," Elliot said.

"Your precious ruins destroyed forever. Nineteen-million years old . . ." Boyd laughed. "Again, you'll be left with nothing! Nothing, at all! Like Nepal. Running around, telling crazy stories nobody believes!" Boyd was angry; he could see that.

"No, actually I think they must be destroyed. Believe it or not, but this isn't archeology. This technology destroyed them, and it would destroy *us*. I believe it would have been best had these ruins never been found," Elliot said. "But you wouldn't understand that."

"Oh, I do. I do. You think I wanted any of this? You think I was . . ." He stopped as Elliot stepped forward; slowly extending his hand to grab the remote control. "Elliot! Professor!"

"Continue. You were just about to tell me a story," Elliot said, and with one flick of his wrist, he snapped the antenna aside, breaking it in two.

Boyd closed his eyes. "You goddamn fool. What have you done?"

"I stopped you from making a mistake." Elliot stepped back again.

Boyd stared at him, then laughed. "You know what? I think it's only fair if you pay for that. I think it's only fair . . ." He took one step forward. "If you pay for that by never knowing if she made it!"

Elliot aimed as Boyd made another small step, his hand hovering over the table, where the gun rested.

"Go ahead. If it has to be like this, let's get over with it," Elliot said.

Boyd pressed his lips together, then his hand moved to the weapon. Elliot pulled the trigger. Boyd wasn't very fast. He never even got close to getting the gun. He was hurled backward and collapsed to the ground. Elliot heard an agonized moan. He snatched the CIA agent's gun and pushed it into his jacket. Then he circled the table.

"You bastard. I knew you didn't have it in you. My second shoulder. You damn bastard," Boyd gasped on the ground. Elliot looked down at him and pointed the gun to his head.

"I knew you couldn't kill me, Professor. Not the noble Elliot Brand!" Boyd hissed, hammering his head against the floor, his arms hanging useless from his body.

"I'm a terrible shot, Boyd. I aimed for your heart," Elliot replied, then grabbed what remained of the remote control, pushing it into his jacket. Limping to the stairs, he heard Boyd yell.

"I need medical help!"

"Yeah," Elliot replied and began his ascent. The man was screaming with primal rage as he put his boots back on and went outside into the snow. He threw the remote control away as he made his way over the battlefield back to Base One. "Please Ashra, don't die," he whispered as Boyd's screams died in the wind.

Chapter 20

Ashra stopped the vehicle right in front of the entrance and saw the red snowcat there. It was at least Miller and McKenzie who had got here. The vehicle had room for a third passenger, but she doubted there had been one. The other soldiers had died defending the depot.

Checking her rifle once more, Ashra grabbed the flashlight from the console next to her and kicked the door open. Holes where bullets had hit the outer hull were everywhere.

She jumped into the snow and hurried to the entrance. Raising her rifle, she entered between the two pillars and decided against switching on her light in the darkness of the corridor. It was warm here now. She pulled the zipper of her jacket down and felt herself begin to sweat. The climate was almost tropical. Ducking, she passed through the darkness until she saw the light from the entry platform. She saw a blurry shape of someone kneeling there. The light from the energy source was now so bright, it made looking into its direction almost impossible. She wished she had brought her sunglasses. Kneeling, she took aim. The shape was small, not the robust frame of Miller. McKenzie. She was working on something. Ashra sucked air in and held it. The bomb. She was working on the bomb.

"McKenzie to Miller, I've armed it. Is the path clear?" she asked and looked up.

"Path clear to waypoint one," Miller replied.

"Good, I'm coming up now," she answered, and Ashra saw her put the belt of the suitcase over her shoulder. Her thumb armed the assault rifle, and she took aim. Then she inched forward. McKenzie heard her and turned around.

"Oh, you're not giving up, hmm?" the soldier said. "Hostile. It's Shah," she reported over the radio.

"Put it down," Ashra demanded. She was pretty confident when she shot; she hit what she wanted—but she would prefer not to shoot at someone carrying a nuclear weapon.

"I think we both know I can't do that," McKenzie replied.

"You said yourself it's a trap. You said yourself that it would overload. So, you think that a bomb next to it will stop it? Miller is an idiot, but you're smart. You're an engineer or something," Ashra said.

McKenzie stared at her. A glimmering silhouette in front of a second white sun. "Actually, I have a PhD in physics," she said.

"Then why are you following his orders? Tell me, McKenzie, if that up there was your nuclear submarine core and you were in the process of overloading it, would it work to detonate a bomb next to it?" Ashra asked.

"No." McKenzie laughed. "It would blow the whole damn thing up. A soldier follows orders. Otherwise, chaos reigns," McKenzie said. "You must understand, you follow orders too."

"Not those that make no sense."

"Then I'm a better soldier than you are," McKenzie said. As Ashra came closer, she saw the woman had her hand on the grip of her submachine gun. Ashra stopped.

"Please, disarm it. We have a better way. Boyd didn't listen, but Elliot has a plan. One not involving nuclear devices. But I'll run out of time. I can't wait any longer for your decision," Ashra said.

"Boyd has . . ."

"He's dead," Ashra snapped. A lie, but a necessary one—or maybe he *was* dead by now.

"Captain, Boyd Green is dead, and the hostile is asking to disarm the bomb. She says she has more effective means to disarm the reactor," McKenzie said into the radio.

"Engage and eliminate hostile. That's an order," was all that Miller replied.

Ashra smirked. "See? I have you right in front of me. Follow this order and you could kill yourself right away. That's what chaos looks like, McKenzie. That's what madness looks like. They're too afraid to be impotent in the face of such technology. They would rather risk mankind than admit how helpless they are. Please. Don't make me do this." Ashra's finger put slight pressure on the trigger. If McKenzie didn't give in, she would have to kill her. She knew that. The two women stared at each other. Then McKenzie dropped her submachine gun and went back to her knees. She flung open the suitcase, and Ashra moved next to her as she turned the main switch to off, then started rotating a seal clockwise. The display counting down from an hour vanished.

"It's disarmed," McKenzie said.

"Thank you. Now get it out of here. Take the snowcat and get as far away from here as possible," Ashra said.

The woman looked up at her and nodded. Then she ripped something from her arm and handed it to Ashra. "The map, you'll need it."

209

Ashra took it, attaching it to her jacket with the tape still glued to it. Taking the suitcases, McKenzie tore the radio from her shoulder and threw it to the ground. Then she took off her backpack and handed it to Ashra.

"What's that?" Ashra asked.

"A parachute. Your only chance," McKenzie said. *Smart idea*, Ashra thought; attaching it to her back while McKenzie closed the locks in front of her chest.

"Miller to McKenzie, report! Report! Dammit!" Ashra checked her watch. An hour and five minutes. She had to move fast. She began to run, holding her assault rifle close to her chest. She jumped the steps as fast as she could, ignoring the abnormal length of each of the stairs as much as possible. She reached the end, and saw the bridge Elliot had mentioned. She understood what he had meant by it not looking trustworthy. She hurried across—if it had held him, it would hold her.

She arrived on the other side of the bridge where the narrow pathway was. Elliot's description had been spot-on. She was just about to push herself forward as a shot hit the wall next to her. She hadn't heard it, so he'd used a silencer. Pressing herself against the wall, she clutched her rifle. A quick look around the corner and another shot hit the stone right beside her head.

He was above.

Ashra took a deep breath. Miller was probably an excellent shot. But so was she. Turning around the corner she switched the rifle to auto fire and pulled the trigger, aiming at the blurry shape moving behind a pillar above. Her shots hammered into the white marble—or whatever it was—as she squeezed through the narrow part. When she arrived on the platform, her gun clicked, and she ejected the magazine with one fluid move, replacing it with the backup. Shots hit the ground next to her, sending debris into every direction. Ashra raised her gun and withdrew as she returned fire, now in short bursts.

Looking aside, she saw the narrow entrance leading to the corridor with the deadly gray ants. She sidestepped, keeping on firing bursts in the direction of Miller, simply to force him into cover so he couldn't shoot her. Wildly, he sent unarmed bursts down, but none of them got close to her. As she slipped through the entrance, she aimed through the scope. He looked like a demon up there in front of the bright white light, tall and muscular. She gave one last burst, and the rifle made a clicking sound. Letting it go, Ashra knew she was out of ammo; she dropped it and withdrew to the corridor.

Miller kept on shooting at the entrance. Had he lost his mind? Possibly, yes. If he had gone up there already, he had passed this corridor, and from all Ashra knew, that was a terrible experience—even with protective gear. Looking aside, she grabbed her flashlight from her belt and sent the light beam down the corridor. The walls were moving. Far away, she saw where Elliot's backpack had once been, now almost completely devoured by the millions of gray ants crawling over it. The little machines had probably not been fed in a long time.

Ashra took the flashbang grenade from her pocket and checked the clock. The ascent had taken her too much time. Forty minutes and there were still quite a few stairs to go after this one, according to Elliot. She just hoped Miller wouldn't have a clean shot toward her when she did. With a handgun, she stood almost no chance in a firefight at that distance. *Forty minutes.* She was running out of time.

With her teeth, she pulled the pin from the grenade, pressed the safety, and covered her eyes with her forearm. Then she let go of it and rolled it into the corridor.

211

Counting back from three, the explosion was unbearably loud. Her ears rang, and all her adrenaline-induced instincts told her to flee, but she forced herself to do the opposite. She ran right to the light that flared up in incredible white brightness. Hectic movements at the walls and under her feet showed it was working. There came a blistering sound as millions of grey ants tried to escape the light.

Ashra took the second grenade and felt a bite on her leg as she pulled the pin off it. She almost lost it, as something else bit her in the cheek. Still holding her forearm against her eyes, she threw the grenade above her and kept on running, as fast as her long sprinter legs could carry her. The second explosion was worse than the first, sending the echo through the entire corridor with such ferocity, it physically hurt her.

She ran up against it, passing the white light and ramming into the wall on the other side. Collapsing, she scrubbed at her face, where she had been bitten and looked back into the corridor. The light there was dying down now, but she was illuminated, lying in the entrance. As she put her hand to the floor, she felt something beneath it cut into her flesh. She withdrew it and saw two syringes lying there. Morphine. Miller had injected morphine into his bloodstream. So he had passed this without any light? Ashra didn't want to know what that would be like. Coughing, she pushed herself up and drew her handgun. She pressed herself against the wall and peered around the corner of the exit, looking above for any signs of Miller—He was nowhere to be seen. Ashra slipped out of the corridor and saw the narrow stairs Elliot had described. She began her ascent.

****

As she finally made it to the top level, she saw she had seven minutes left. She had been faster, making good time. She took the luxury to kneel behind a pillar, lurking around the corner. The

212

light up here was so bright she couldn't see a thing. Even looking for a second caused her eyes to be branded with white for a long time afterwards. tearing her scarf off, she tied it around her eyes, then took strips of inner lining out of her jacket, pushing it between her makeshift blindfold and her eyes. It was the best she could do to counter the light.

She knew pretty much where she had to go. Straight until she reached the pillar, then to the left until she found stairs. Carefully, still holding her gun in both hands, she made her way around the corner. Even with the protection for her eyes, some light seemed to come through. She pressed her eyes closed and moved forward, her fingers desperately clinging to the gun. It wasn't an effective weapon if you couldn't see, but it made her feel less vulnerable. She had no idea how far she had got on the bridge, maybe halfway, when she heard the steps. She stopped right away and dropped to one knee. *Miller.* It had to be Miller. He was up here. Awaiting her in the light. She raised her gun, and as she heard steps again, she fired three quick shots in that direction, each a little further left than the one before.

Kneeling, she listened. No gasping, no moaning. She must have missed him. Confirmation came as she was suddenly ripped from the ground and hammered into the floor. She felt one of her left ribs break and gasped in pain. Then she realized what a mistake that had been and rolled to the side, as a foot stomped where her head had been. Not making a sound, she crawled back and heard a scream that barely sounded human anymore. It seemed to be an expression of all the anger in the world.

She took the chance and slid forward, letting her leg snap out, as she did a roundhouse kick at the height of his legs. She felt the impact as her knee hit him and the body of the man crashed down. Ashra jumped up and pointed the gun to the ground, pulling the trigger. After two shots, a click was heard, and the magazine automatically ejected. She hadn't checked how many bullets she had left when she had taken it from the soldier—an amateur mistake she would have to be angry about later. Now, she went to one knee and groped forward. Miller wasn't lying there. He had escaped. Cursing silently, Ashra stayed on her knee and awaited the next attack. It didn't come. She heard a gasp, then groaning.

"I'll killlll youuu!" Miller yelled.

Ashra decided she wasn't going to wait for that. She moved forward as Miller screamed behind her. She wasn't sure if she was still going in the right direction and expected to fall off the edge of the bridge any second as she had lost orientation. Instead, her hands touched the vibrating, warm wall of the pillar.

She laughed in relief. Left. Slowly, she stepped to the left, and her feet suddenly felt the platform vanish. Gently putting her foot down, she felt ground again. Stairs. The stairs leading to the control room. As fast as her blindness allowed, she made her way down there, then felt the entrance. Ripping off her blindfold, she blinked as her eyes adjusted to the new state of being able to see again. Even in her blurry vision she saw exactly what Elliot had described. A room full of blue crystals. Blue lines of light projected between them, changing locations. She stumbled forward and grabbed one. It moved out of its position right away. Letting it fall to the ground, she picked another and then another, ripping them out as fast as she could, as her eyes began slowly focusing again. She saw the blue light beams change location rapidly as she kept on pulling them out. A quick look at her watch showed she had about two minutes left. Two minutes and three seconds to be precise—if the attack happened on time.

Frenziedly, she kept on ripping them out, crawling on the ledge on which the crystals were embedded. She saw the first beams freeze, unable to find a new location anymore. It wasn't fast enough though. She knew it probably had to be Plan B. She crawled back and set her feet down, reaching into her jacket. She withdrew the explosive hand grenade she had brought. She would regret this moment. She was suddenly grabbed from behind, an arm around her neck, and lifted into the air. Gasping for air, she let go of the grenade, and still unarmed, it fell to the ground between the blue crystals covering most of the floor.

Miller was incredibly strong, almost breaking her neck with the sheer force by which he pressed her against himself. Struggling on her feet, she tried to clear her head. The lack of oxygen made you panic, and if you panicked, you were dead. Her hands reached out and she felt one of the crystals. She took it in both hands, pressed her leg against the ledge, and pushed herself away from it.

Miller stumbled back, and just as he regained his footing, she rammed the crystal up, hammering it with both hands into his skull.

He cried out and repeated the action again. Finally, he let go of her and she slid to the ground. Desperately soaking in air, she grabbed the ledge to pull herself up again, the crystal still in one hand. She looked up and saw Miller for the first time clearly since they had arrived here. She gasped. His face was mostly eaten away, his flesh lying bare as his skin was completely gone below the nose. His teeth had mostly fallen out. His nose was eaten away. And then there were his eyes. Burned into a brilliant white, he spread his arms to search for her. From his chest a bullet wound was bleeding. With the double dose of morphine in his blood, he seemed not to feel any pain.

Ashra gasped again and raised the crystal once more. Miller had heard the gasp, and with a speed she hadn't thought possible for such a flayed body, he rammed against her, trying to grab her. Ashra hammered the crystal on his head but didn't have enough power at this short distance. He ripped her off her feet and tossed her into the water like a doll. Her broken rib sent a wave of pain through her as she landed on the ground. Her back hurt, her arms felt as if they could barely move anymore. Then she saw something shift from the side of her vision, and with the last strength she had, she pushed herself up and away, as Miller jumped right where she had been lying, hammering his fists into the ground. She was sure she heard his hands break, but he didn't seem to care anymore. Screaming out in frustration, he turned and crawled toward her. Ashra pulled her leg to her body and hammered a kick into his face. It made him collapse for a moment, but he reared up again right away. Jumping up, Ashra stepped aside and he rammed into the wall where he had suspected her. There he stayed, breathing as heavy as her, and a lower, more growling scream came from his mouth.

"I have . . . rrrrrh!" he gasped, as if his tongue had been eaten away by the gray ants, too.

Ashra looked at her watch. *Thirty seconds.* Her eyes wandered over the ground, and between a pile of crystals she saw the grenade. She picked it up as Miller charged again. This time, she was prepared and turned with the strength she had left, kicking out right at his throat. The man collapsed and gasped for air, holding his throat.

"I'm sorry," Ashra said and pulled the pin from the grenade. Holding the safety down still, she stepped back, then tossed the grenade through the entrance into the control room. Then she turned and began to run. She ran straight to the edge, the light engulfing her. The explosion behind her was so loud it echoed through the entire cave that contained the city. The shockwave ripped her off her feet and sent her flying over the edge of the small gangway leading to the control room.

Ashra grabbed the release of the parachute and ripped it down. The parachute opened just as her fall began. Where she was attached by her shoulders, it sent waves of pain through her broken rib. She began to glide instead of falling. She saw the platform on the other side and the clock at her arm started beeping. *Time was up.* She could only hope the Russians were late. The cave grew darker, long shadows casting on the walls, and with one last look back, she saw the giant energy sphere on top of the pillar slowly dwarf, revealing the beams circling around it again that had been completely consumed before. Elliot had been right—of course, he had.

Before she could enjoy her triumph, a rumbling went through the cave. Then another. Holding tight to the parachute, she saw the platform coming closer as parts of the ceiling collapsed and crashed into the waters below. A flash of light, and there came a thundering sound as a missile hit the pillar and it broke apart. Explosions filled the entire cave, and a wall of fire began to form at her back, the heat wave carrying her forward and burning her skin. Then the shockwave arrived, and she felt the push forward with a speed she couldn't control. Covering her head, she knew she wouldn't land, but *crash* into the platform that was coming closer way too fast now. Screaming, she closed her eyes and awaited impact. As it came, her world was engulfed by darkness.

****

Ashra's eyes opened, and the first thing she felt was a humming in her head, followed by the cold of snow. She was lying there. She was also alive. She knew this because every bone in her body ached. Over her, McKenzie's face appeared.

"You?" Ashra asked.

"Got you out of there before the whole thing came down," she said.

Ashra looked to the side. The entire rift that had contained the ruins was gone now, collapsed under the bombardment of the Russians. She lay next to the snowcat in the snow.

"I would guess you have a concussion, some broken ribs, and God knows what, but you're alive," McKenzie summarized her patient's status.

Ashra smiled. "Did I not tell you to get away from there?"

"Yeah, been hanging out too much with you guys, I'm afraid. Got really bad at following orders and all that," McKenzie said; she couldn't hold back a laugh, that Ashra joined her in.

"You did it? I mean, the reactor?" McKenzie asked.

"Otherwise we wouldn't be here."

"Well then, let's see if we can get you back to the base. I guess we have a man there who would like to tell you what a great job you did," McKenzie said. "If you don't mind, I'll take the nuke."

Ashra looked aside and saw the suitcase still lay there.

"By any means," she replied.

Chapter 21

Elliot forced himself up as he saw the snowcat arrive. Swelling, hard tears filled his eyes, as he saw what he had considered impossible—limping worse than him, battered and covered in dust—Ashra climbed out of it.

She laughed at him, and he made his way over to her, pulling her into a tight embrace.

"Elliot, I'm pretty sure some of these ribs are actually broken," Ashra whispered, but slung her arms around him.

"I saw the explosion. How the hell did you get out of there?" he asked as he parted from her.

"Flying," she said.

Elliot laughed, not really caring for any of the details. For now, he was nothing but grateful she was alive. He leaned forward and kissed her. Ashra returned the kiss but then gasped as she felt his hands at her neck.

"What?"

"Even that hurts." Ashra winced.

"Shall I stop?"

"Hell no. Never again," Ashra grinned at him as he kissed her again. He could have continued for hours, had he not heard the door of the passenger's side of the snowcat close. McKenzie returned his gaze, without showing the slightest emotion.

219

"I'll bring this to safety, I guess." She held up the suitcase, and Elliot nodded. He watched as she trotted over to the depot.

"She did the right thing," Ashra leaned against Elliot, her arms slung around him. "Can we get in? I've had enough of the cold."

"In a minute, okay? One more thing I need to do," Elliot turned, revealing the campfire he had made. He stepped over and grabbed the box next to it, drawing the last piece of his collection out of it—the sample of the gray ants.

"What are you doing there?" Ashra asked.

"Burning it all," Elliot said. He threw the vial into the fire and turned to Ashra. "The tapes, laptops, samples, I burned everything."

"Why? Those were invaluable for your—"

"Research? Shall I tell the world there's an energy source like this buried under the ice? What will happen? Wars will be fought over it, and in the end we humans will weaponize it. We always do. I've studied the past long enough to know that. Those little things, I think they were responsible for the end of that civilization. So why would I want to replicate them? Why would I want anyone to do that?" He looked at Ashra, and she nodded in understanding.

"That must be hard, anyway." She sighed.

"Hardest thing I've ever done."

"They're still down there, aren't they?"

"I guess they are. What we saw was only the part of the ruins where the ice melted away. Frozen down there in the dark . . . they're still there, yes."

220

"How do we keep anyone from looking for them?"

"We need to coordinate our stories. We need to lie about what we found." He knew it violated every principle as a scientist, but this wasn't a scientific question. His job was to research the past, not change the future. "I think I've been wrong all along. The Ancients, these Ancestors. They died out long ago, and for a reason. It's probably a bad idea to try and bring anything from them back," Elliot said more to himself than to her.

"Do you seriously mean that?"

"Every word." Elliot took Ashra's hand. "Don't leave me again."

"I . . . I don't know what to say, Elliot. I . . ." She shook her head.

Then Elliot saw something was wrong. She opened her mouth, but no sound came out of it, almost as if she had lost command over her voice. Her eyes began to roll back, and he felt her legs give out. He caught her as she slid to the ground. Her body was shaking now. Spasms went through it.

"Ashra! Ashra, talk to me!" Elliot yelled as he saw her head roll aside. Then the spasms stopped, and she lay still in the snow in front of him. Elliot turned to the depot and started shouting. It was the same word he repeated again and again. "Help! Help!"

****

A month had passed since the rescue team had got them out of the remains of the base camp in Antarctica. Elliot had alternated between the interrogation cells of the CIA and the hospital Ashra had been brought to. He had only cooperated under the condition he could see her and hadn't left her side for longer than an hour. Once the interrogations winded down, he had taken a motel on the opposite side of the street and spent every waking hour with her. Three surgeries had been performed, but none of the doctors told him anything. He wasn't a relative, after all. So all he could do was hold her hand and wait for her to wake up. A nurse who saw how close they were and how worried he was, had told him she would eventually. Only when, nobody knew. He gazed at her, now with a shaven head, looking weakened and vulnerable. He stared at her for an entire month, waiting for her to wake up.

When the man approached, he didn't even hear him. The lack of sleep had taken its toll.

"You must be Professor Brand," the man said with a gentle voice, and Elliot's head craned up. An elderly Nepalese man of small build stood there, wearing glasses, a hat and a perfectly tailored three-piece suit.

"I'm her uncle." He stepped forward, offering his hand.

"Yes, I'm the Professor." Elliot got up, shaking the man's hand.

"The head wound was bad they said, but they don't expect any long-term effects. That's what they told me."

"They haven't told me anything." Elliot sighed and sat down again.

"She's young and strong. She'll be the old Ashra eventually, but it'll need time. Recovery, training." The uncle who hadn't mentioned his name, sat down on the only other chair in the room.

"I'll be there for her."

"I think we should talk about that. It's actually the reason why I came here." He took his glasses off and polished them with a handkerchief.

"Ah." Elliot looked at the harmless-looking elderly man and nodded. "I remember she told me her job had a tradition in her family. Her uncle was in the same line of work. That uncle is you I assume?"

"Yes, that uncle would be me." The elderly man confirmed. "You know, Professor Brand, you had three days before the rescue came. We all are lucky Ashra was still alive by then. A lot of time to coordinate your stories, of course. I read the reports. A courtesy of the Americans after we not only almost lost one of our own, but also through one of their agents clearly having lost his mind. I must say an interesting read. A good story that makes perfect sense. A little too perfect maybe."

"It's the truth."

"It probably contradicts what the CIA officer has to say."

"He's not a credible source, I assume." Elliot felt uneasy now, folding his arms instinctively, checking Ashra with a quick look.

"Well, someone considers him credible enough to check your story. There's a man down the corridor, posing as a security guard? From what I saw, I'd say he's not." The uncle leaned forward. "I heard many stories over the years, Professor. True ones and lies. Often what is a matter of perspective. So I guess our cousins from Langley are very eager to get their hands on my niece and ask her for her story. Did you have time to coordinate your story with her? Hmm?" The elderly man put his glasses back on, and Elliot remained silent.

"Professor, you put her into a very difficult situation. If she tells the truth, it could be very dangerous for you. If she lies, it could be very dangerous for her. Anyway, someone is in danger. I can't imagine that to be in your interest, right?"

223

Elliot kept on staring at him. He knew where this was going, and he hated it. But he also knew he was playing a very dangerous game here, and this man was probably right.

"So what are you suggesting?" Elliot finally asked.

"She needs medical attention. We'll take good care of one of our own, Professor. Maybe it's time to bring her home. Even the CIA can't deny us to bring one of our own home, especially not when she came to harm while helping them out." Her uncle stood up.

"You don't need my approval for that, do you?"

"No, Professor, I don't. But out of appreciation for all you did and what you mean to her, I decided to ask for permission." The uncle came closer to the bed and gently stroked Ashra's shaved head. "So do I have your permission to bring her home, Professor?"

Elliot looked at the elderly man, then his eyes went to Ashra. He disliked nothing more than the idea of losing her again. But she had once decided against him. Who said if she had a choice she would not do the same again right now? That and obviously her uncle was right. In the US, she would be questioned, and that would bring her into a very uncomfortable position.

"Okay," Elliot said and let go of her hand.

"Thank you." Then he stepped back from her and turned to leave. "One more thing. I need to ask. What did you find out there? In Antarctica?"

Elliot gave a deep sigh. "Old stones, really old stones. Fascinating stuff, I have to say. But not . . . really . . . much left. After all those years."

Ashra's uncle smiled a little. "Then you'll be out there in no time, investigating them?"

"The caves collapsed. That and there was a high amount of radioactivity that makes investigating them quite dangerous. That's why the satellites picked up those electro-magnetic fields." Elliot had told the story a thousand times by now. Long form, short form. Every shape and size a story could have.

"That's regrettable." The uncle walked to the door. "But a good story. Stick to it. I believe the Americans bought it. They probably want a reason to not go back, so . . . good luck." He sent one last smile across the room, then vanished. Elliot sat down next to the unconscious Ashra and picked up her hand again. He knew she would be taken away soon; and even if she wouldn't wake up, the only thing he could do now, was to enjoy the time they had together.

THE END

****

Get access to news, background information and exclusive stories:

Subscribe to my newsletter now!
Just write a mail to **FalkNewsletter@gmail.com**
with the subject: SUBSCRIBE

THE ADVENTURE CONTINUES . . .

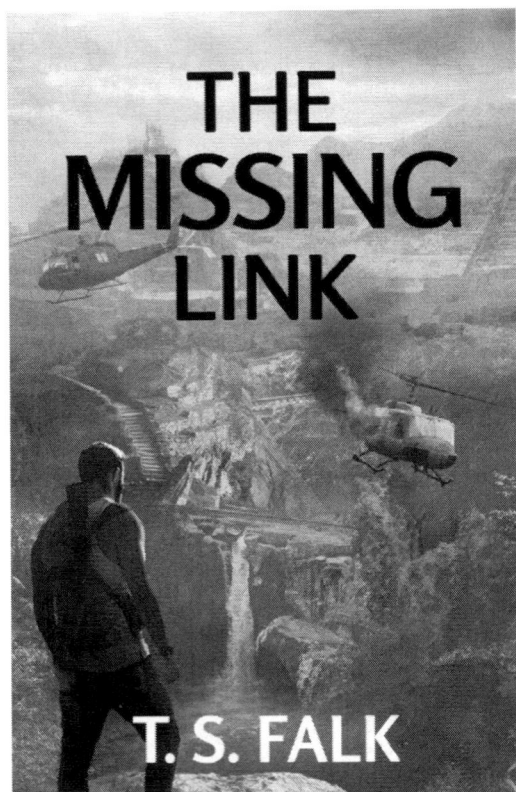

ONLY AVAILABLE ON AMAZON

Enjoy This Book?
You Can Make A Difference.

If you like what you just read, I would kindly ask you for a favor, my dear reader.

For you, it would be a few minutes of your time, but for me, it would mean the world if you head over to Amazon and write a review with your honest opinion about my novel. Even a short review helps. My eternal gratitude would be yours.

Many thanks in advance!

Yours,

T.S. Falk

Printed in Great Britain
by Amazon